UNFINISHED
Business

Dedication

A Special thank you to my girls Angie, Debbie, Lee and Charlotte for always having my back and reading my stories. My cousin Heather deserves a special mention as she's an amazing person who is always willing to help. I wish you find someone who makes you smile, and makes you feel loved the way you deserve. To Abbie, Sue, Crystal, Lisa, Leslie, Tammy and Jennifer, and everyone else who helped me with this emotional project, thank you for your patience, kind words, and support.

In dedication and memory of my mother who was an amazing woman and loved by many. Life continually dealt her an unfair hand but despite her struggles she was the strongest woman I've ever known. Her passing was sudden and unexpected and I can't stop thinking about all the things we were going to do because we thought we had more time with her. I miss her everyday but I find comfort in knowing she's finally with dad and they are both always watching over us. Thank you for everything you taught me and how you loved your grandsons and great-grandson unconditionally.

Unfinished Business

The crowd erupts in cheers as the final whistle blows, and the young men leave the lacrosse field with a glorious playoff victory. My son ignores me when I stand and wave as he exits the arena. Noticing my disappointment, my mother places her hand on my arm.

"He's a teenage boy," she reminds me.

I gather my things, and we head to the lobby to wait for him. My eyes are drawn to an obnoxiously large real estate ad hanging in the arena. After all these years, I'm still a sucker for those chestnut brown eyes. It's amazing that I've been able to avoid running into him since it seems like he sponsors every sport my kid plays.

My mom looks up, curious about what I'm staring at. She smiles. "I ran into him a few weeks ago at the market."

It's funny how sometimes her Irish brogue comes across so pronounced. She's been in Canada for so many years, most times, I can hardly detect it. When I can, it makes me think of my dad, who was barely comprehensible when he was angry. I always knew I was in trouble if the yelling was in Irish. I pretend her news doesn't faze me. "You didn't mention it."

"I didn't? I meant to. You used to have so much fun together. You should call him."

My pulse quickens. "We're not teenagers anymore, Mom." As the team starts to appear one by one in the lobby, they're greeted by their families. "Do you think it bothers him?"

"That you never explored if there could be something long-lasting between you?"

She had to go there. "No, mom. I'm not talking about Alex."

"Who are you talking about, dear?"

"Jack. I wonder if it bothers him seeing all the other boys celebrating with their fathers and grandfathers and..." I pause.

"And he's stuck with just you and me?"

"He was so young when his father picked up and moved away, and then the only grandfather he knew passed away."

"He seems fine to me."

"He needs a positive male role model in his life. I'm sure that's why he's waffling on college choices."

"Maya," she interrupts. "All your overthinking must make you exhausted. Maybe he just hasn't decided what he wants to do yet."

Jack pushes his way through the crowd, and I smile as I throw my arms around him. "Great job, son. Congratulations!"

He pulls himself out of my arms and politely endures the same greeting from my mother.

"Let's go out for dinner," she says with excitement. "Anywhere you want to go."

I'm relieved the invitation comes from her since he's less likely to turn down his grandma. One of his teammates walks past and holds up his hand for a high-five.

"Are you coming to Mark's house? Everyone is going. There's pizza and video games, and they have an indoor pool."

I raise a brow and quickly offer an acceptable compromise. "I can drop you off after we go out for dinner."

He looks at my mom with great disappointment, and as usual, she gives in. "It's okay, Jack. Go with your friends. We can celebrate another time."

He doesn't wait for my acknowledgement or approval. "I love you, Grandma," he says excitedly as he calls out to his friend and tries to catch up.

"Jack! WAIT!" I holler. My shoulders fall, and I sigh as I look down at the giant bag of smelly lacrosse equipment. "Put your equipment in the car," I grunt as I lift the heavy bag. "Awesome." It nearly pulls me over as I try to swing it over my shoulder. My ninety-pound mother reaches out to steady me as if there was any way she could stop me from tipping over.

"Need some help?"

The sound of his voice causes the hair on the back of my neck to stand.

"Alex," my mother says excitedly. "Yes, dear. We're in a bit of a pickle."

"It's okay, Mom. I've got it." I try to hide the strain the added weight is putting on me. I'd rather get a hernia than accept help from Alex Thomas.

He chuckles as he lifts the heavy bag from my shoulder as if it was full of feathers. "I see you haven't changed any in fifteen years."

"Seventeen," I blurt out in a failed attempt at a witty comeback. My mother's brow furrows and I shrug, even more annoyed by her censure.

Alex ignores my comment and directs his conversation toward my mother. "Let me help you get this to the car."

"Thank you, dear. You look handsome as usual. I love the beard. What are you doing here?"

I raise a brow. I swear she's flirting with him.

"I sponsor the team." He nods in the direction of the sign. "I tried to get to all the games, but I wouldn't miss the championship for anything. I don't remember it being so rough when I played. Maybe I'm just getting soft in my old age."

"The game hasn't changed." I ignore my mother's look of disapproval.

Mom looks perplexed. "Don't you think it's strange we haven't run into each other before now?"

I mumble quietly under my breath. "Because we've been avoiding each other for seventeen years. It's not that hard to figure out."

"What did you say, Maya?"

"Nothing."

"I guess we're always sitting in different parts of the arena." He follows us through the parking lot. "Your boy is a fantastic player. There's a fire in him when he has the ball."

"How do you know which kid is mine?" I ask suspiciously.

He quirks an annoying grin. "His jersey number is on his bag."

Feeling stupid, I stop at the rear of my SUV and open the lift gate.

"And I've seen you together from the other side of the field." Alex effortlessly swings the bag in and steps back out of the way as I close it. AHA! So, he did know I was at the games. There's a strange look of reverence on his face when I turn to thank him, and it throws me off-guard. I stumble for words and shake my head to get my thoughts straight. "Thank you."

"It was great to see you again."

I'm distracted as a vehicle full of loud and excited teenagers drives past, and Jack glances at us through the open window. I begin to raise my hand to wave and stop myself.

"We're going out for supper if you care to join us," my mother adds.

"Thank you, but I'm showing a house to a buyer in twenty minutes."

I feel a strange combination of relief and disappointment.

"Well, don't be a stranger," my mother says. "Come by and visit. You know where to find me."

Alex laughs aloud once. "Yes, ma'am. I will."

"I like my tea, milk in first, no sugar, bag left in,"

She says with a smile. "They never get it right at those drive-thru places."

He shuts off the alarm that springs to life on his phone. "I've got to run. Enjoy your supper."

I can't help myself. I glance over my shoulder as he walks away. I'm embarrassed when he does the same and finds me looking.

I jump into the SUV and try to act composed as I adjust my seatbelt.

My mother glances sideways and smiles at my failed attempt to look indifferent. "Well, that was a pleasant surprise."

I put the vehicle in drive and pull into traffic. "It was a surprise, but I'm not sure it was pleasant."

"Maya, I don't know who you think you're fooling. But it's not me."

"How about we discuss where we're going for dinner instead?"

"Fine. Nothing too fancy. I haven't had much of an appetite lately."

"Well, that's something I can never complain about. I never seem to lose my appetite. How about we go to Lucy's Bistro?"

"That sounds wonderful."

Luckily, there's no wait time at the family restaurant where we frequently eat, so they are able to seat us right away. My brow creases with concern when my mom orders only soup. "What's going on with you?" I ask when the waitress leaves the table.

"I'm fine."

"You look tired, and I've never known you not to have an appetite. Especially when someone else is paying."

"My body doesn't need as much fuel as it used to because I don't do anything."

I'm concerned. "When was the last time you saw your doctor?"

"Oh, for heaven's sake, Maya. I'm not sick. Just old. Let it go. Let's talk about something else."

"Anything but Alex."

She frowns. "Okay, but you have to admit he looks ruggedly handsome."

I tilt my head to the side. "I said anything but Alex."

She sighs loudly in protest. "How is your job?"

I lean back and relax more. "It's good. I get to torture people for a living and get paid for it."

"I wouldn't call physiotherapy torture."

"You would if you heard all the moaning, groaning and complaining."

"I think it's wonderful you help people feel better. I'm very proud of you."

I pause and reflect on her statement. "Thanks, Mom."

"Your son will do wonderful things with his life, as well. Stop pushing him and let him discover what he's passionate about."

I nod. "Message received. Speaking of messages...have you heard from any of your other children lately?"

"I spoke to your sister June a few weeks ago."

"Oh?"

"Or was it a few months ago? I'm not sure."

Her hand trembles as she tries to lift her cup to her mouth. Knowing she can't hide it from me now, she places it on the table. "I think it's time for me to get home. I'm cold, and I'm starting to feel tired."

When she stands, I help her with her sweater and let her hold my arm while we walk to the car.

Few words are spoken on the way home. I help her out of the SUV and to the front door. She struggles with her keys. It's hard to watch. I suppose that's how it is for most people when their parents reach their twilight years. It's hard to watch them slow down and become weaker. More fragile. "Are you sure you're feeling okay? I can stay if you want. Jack's getting a ride home with his friend, so I don't have to be anywhere."

"Not necessary. I'm going to get ready for bed and watch the television for a few hours."

I make sure she's in the door, and the lights are on before leaving. As I get into my SUV, I turn on my Bluetooth. "Call June." It immediately goes to voicemail, and I'm frustrated. I'm sure she just declined my call.

"Hi, it's Maya. Give me a call when you have time. I need to talk to you about Mom."

I'm not sure why I left a message. She never calls me back. It aggravates me that my siblings think moving out of town exempts them from checking in on the rest of the family. I know life gets busy, so they can't visit often, but there's no reason they can't manage a phone call now and then.

My brother, Brian, has always gotten a free pass with my mom. She makes excuses for him when he doesn't call or blows off family events. Maybe it's her old-school way of thinking that the female children are the ones who look after their parents while the male children are too busy providing and looking after their own families.

It frustrates me. The rest of us have families to look after as well. I'm trying to do it alone. I know there's no point in trying to get Brian on the phone, so I text him to let him know his mother would like to hear from him. He'll ignore me as well, I'm sure.

I'm one hundred percent certain that my youngest sister Jennifer has her phone in her hand twenty-four seven. "Call Jennifer."

She answers on the first ring. "Hello, sister."

"Hi, Jen. How are you?"

"Not doing too bad. Work is crazy right now. I'm trying to balance two projects simultaneously, and a new one is starting shortly."

"I don't know how you do it with three children under the age of six."

"I don't sleep."

"I'm not surprised. Listen, I had dinner with Mom tonight. I'm worried about her."

"What's up?"

"She's got no appetite, and she looks drained. She says she's fine, but I don't think she's telling me the truth."

"Do you think she's sick?"

"I don't know."

"Have you talked to June and Brian about it?"

"I left messages, but they never call me back."

"That's nothing new."

"True. I was hoping maybe if you talked to her, you might get more out of her."

"There's no way I have time to visit right now. Oh, shoot. There's a call coming in that I have to take. I've got to go, but I'll try to call her tomorrow between meetings."

She hangs up without even saying goodbye.

"I might as well be an only child," I growl as I pull into my driveway.

The house is dark and quiet. I pour myself a glass of wine and turn on the television. There's a romance movie marathon just beginning. Usually, I'd turn it off and listen to music, but tonight, I'm in a sentimental mood.

The door slams as Jack rushes down the hallway. "I'm home," he hollers, already halfway up the stairs.

"Did you have a good time?" I yell.

"The guys are starting an online campaign on our favourite video game, and I need to sign in." His door slams and I raise my glass in the air. "I had a nice dinner with Grandma," I say sarcastically.

I pull a blanket over my legs and settle in.

Chapter Two

I sit at the kitchen table and enjoy a peaceful morning with a cup of coffee. Flipping through the pages of the local newspaper, I catch up on all the local events and news. Alex is on every page. Volunteering, sponsoring...advertising. I chuckle. He made growing up in a small town an incredible adventure. It's a miracle I managed to avoid him all these years.

Behind me, it sounds like a stampede is coming down the stairs.

"Good morning," I say as Jack stomps past me and swings open a cupboard door to get a cereal bowl. "You didn't answer my question last night. Did you have fun at your friend's house?"

The cereal sounds like marbles bouncing around in the bowl as he pours it out of the box from a foot above. "Yeah."

I pause, waiting for him to expand, but I suppose that's too much to expect from a teenage boy who has never been elaborate with details. "Please don't leave me to deal with your smelly equipment next time."

"Sorry." He pulls out a chair and sits beside me. "I was excited, and I wasn't thinking."

"I got that."

"Who was the guy you were talking to in the parking lot?"

"Just a guy who helped us get the bag to the SUV."

He looks at me suspiciously, and I don't know why my face flushes.

"Just some guy?"

"He's one of the team sponsors. He and I grew up together. His parents lived around the corner from Grandma."

He shoves cereal into his mouth in an unusually aggressive manner. "Is there something wrong?" I ask.

He lifts the bowl to his mouth and drinks the last of the milk. "I don't know." He gets to his feet to put his dishes in the sink. "You know how you say sometimes you get feelings about things?"

I nod. I've had intuitive moments since I was a little girl. When I was a teenager, they terrified me. I never really understood it until I was older. My siblings don't seem to share the gift if you can call it that. If they do, they've kept it a secret.

I wonder if what Jack experienced was jealousy or concern. He's never seen me with a man other than his father. He's not a child anymore. I decide not to elaborate on the topic of Alex to avoid any conversation that might lead to the whole truth. I've put that all behind me. "What are your plans for today?"

"I don't know." He shrugs. "Chill."

"I'm going to visit Grandma. She wasn't feeling well last night, and I want to check on her. Why don't you come with me? She did you a solid last night. I would have made you go to dinner."

There's an aggravated tone in his voice. "Clearly, Grandma loves me more than you."

"All the more reason to go and visit with her now."

"When are you going?"

"Now."

"Right now?"

"Yes, right now. Have you got other plans at ten in the morning?"

"No, but..."

"Good. Let's go."

If I had a dollar for every time I annoyed my son, I could retire a rich woman today. We make the drive in silence while he focuses on his phone.

He looks up as we round the corner. "Somebody is here."

"Crap."

"What's wrong?"

I recognize the vehicle. "Nothing. Do you think you could put away the brooding expression when you see your grandma?" I ask of him as we pull into the driveway. "She doesn't need to feel like you're being forced to visit."

He expels a frustrated breath. "Yes, ma'am."

On the way to the front door, Jack notices the back gate is open. "She must be in the yard."

The walkway along the side of the house is bright and full of life as the blooms from the rose bushes flourish and thrive, creating a strong contrast with the faded, weather-beaten brick house.

As we approach the back patio, the hair on the back of my neck stands on end. Jack lowers his brow when he hears a man's voice. I force myself to keep walking.

My mother's face lights up when she sees us. "Maya! Jack! My goodness. I wasn't expecting so many visitors this morning."

I lean down and kiss her on the cheek. "Good morning, Mom. I just wanted to pop in to make sure you're feeling better."

Alex gets to his feet and extends his hand. "Hi, Jack. I'm Alex. I sponsor your lacrosse team. You played a fantastic game yesterday."

Jack accepts his outstretched hand. "Thank you. I hear you used to live in Grandma's neighbourhood."

Alex raises a brow and quickly gives me a side glance. "Well, yes. I still do. Your mom and I were friends once," he says with a grin.

"We went to school together," I add, feeling awkward. Alex gives me his signature boyish grin, and for a split second, I contemplate hitting him in the face with the garden shovel located conveniently to my right. My mother begins to speak, pulling me out of my fantasy.

"I was just telling Alex how each different type of rose has a unique fragrance. Not all roses smell the same."

"Grandma knows them all with her eyes closed," Jack says proudly.

My mom blushes. "Oh," she says with a small laugh. "Well, I used to, but when you get older, sense of smell is one of the things that goes."

I'm relieved she has a little more colour to her skin than yesterday.

"Let's try one." Jack grins and darts off to the side of the house. "Close your eyes, Grams," he says, returning with his hand behind his back.

I can see the excitement on her face as she willingly closes her eyes and lifts her nose higher, preparing herself. Jack places a small pink bud an inch away from her nose. She takes a deep, slow breath and smiles. "Polyantha." She opens her eyes. "The fairy rose. Your grandfather bought me a fairy rose bush for our first wedding anniversary."

Jack passes the rose to Alex so we can enjoy the fragrance. "I'm impressed." He lifts it to his nose and then passes it to me.

"Money was tight back then, and they had four kids to raise. So, she forbade him from wasting money on things like frivolous anniversary and birthday gifts. To make up for it, whenever he had a little extra money put aside, he bought her a new rose bush for the garden."

My mom looks around the garden of blossoms. "Many of them have been here over fifty years. Sometimes, they bloom and grow effortlessly." She turns her gaze toward us with an impassive look. "Sometimes they need a lot of attention and care to keep them thriving."

Alex leans slightly toward me and whispers. "I think that's directed at us."

"Undoubtedly," I confirm.

"My late husband used to say we brought the magic of Ireland with us, and it helped our garden thrive." She leans back in her chair. "I'm feeling a wee bit hungry. Maya, would you mind getting me a little snack?"

"Sure, Mom. Are you ready to go in?"

"Not yet. The sun feels good on these old bones."

I frown and look at Alex. "Lunch in the garden then."

"Do you want some help?"

"Nope, I can throw together some ham sandwiches all by myself."

He acknowledges my sarcasm. "Still mad at me, eh?"

I ignore him. "Jack, I noticed some garden tools lying around. Could you gather them up and put them in the shed before they start to rust." I walk toward the house and hear them talking as I go.

"What was that about?" Jack asks, confused.

Alex chuckles, and I know he's watching me. I can feel his eyes on me. "A mistake I made many years ago. That girl can hold a grudge."

"Tell me about it," I hear Jack say as I enter the house.

Still concerned about my mom, I watch through the kitchen window while pulling stuff out of the fridge to throw together for a quick lunch. Jack emerges from the garden shed with a football, and Alex's face lights up. All lunch production stops as I become distracted watching Alex and Jack toss a football across the yard. For more than a few moments, I ponder how wonderful our lives might have been if things had worked out differently. Not that I didn't love

Jack's father. He came in and swept me off my feet when I felt very vulnerable. It all happened so fast, and Alex let me go effortlessly, ending a relationship that never really started.

Nine months after I met Kevin, Jack was born. I think we both realized that we didn't have much in common after we got married. That, together with the pressures of being new parents and...well, adulting in general, strained our relationship until we slowly grew apart. He left when Jack was four.

A crow sits on a branch a few feet away from the window. His caw demands my attention. His appearance is a sign from the universe that I don't understand yet. Sadness washes over me, and I take a breath, then wipe a tear from my eye as I pull myself together and throw everything on a tray.

As I walk into the yard, Alex tosses the football and then heads toward me.

"Here, let me help."

He looks concerned as he takes the tray out of my hands. "Is everything okay?"

I lower my eyes to hide the redness and force a smile. "Yes, I was just cutting an onion."

He tilts his head and smirks. "You know, I can still tell when you're lying to me."

Annoyed, I roll my eyes before following him. I could have come up with something better since there is no onion on the tray I brought out.

I can tell my mom is equally enjoying the snack and the company. I have often asked her to sell the house and move in with Jack and me. There's no reason for her to be living here alone. I suppose she's just not ready yet since she always turns me down. I'm unsure if she thinks she'll lose her independence or doesn't want to lose her connection to my dad and the garden at this home.

"How are your parents?" I ask Alex between mouthfuls.

"They're great. They sold the house and are living their best lives travelling the world."

"Really? That's incredible at their age."

He wipes the corner of his mouth with the back of his hand. "They bought a motorhome, and they're driving it from coast to coast."

My mom tries to place her drink beside her and nearly misses the table. "I'm exhausted just thinking about it."

"Yes, they're lucky to have reasonably good health and mobility still. They always wanted to travel. They have a timeshare in Florida, and from there, they jump on cruise ships whenever they feel like a break from driving."

"Good for them," I say, impressed.

"For now, we've used my address as their permanent residence, and I have an in-law suite, so if they ever need a place to stay that's *not* mobile, they'll stay with me."

"Did you hear that, Mom? Alex's parents live with him."

"I believe what he said was they visit occasionally, Maya. There's a big difference."

20

"If you sold the house, you could go on cruises. Just saying."

"Let it go, dear."

I grimace. "I hear that a lot."

Alex tries to hide a smile as he helps me gather up the garbage. "She's a tough cookie."

"Mmmhmm. Now you know where I get it from."

"Oh, for heaven's sake," I overhear my mom say to Jack. "Do they think I'm so old I can't hear them? Your mother takes stubbornness to a whole new level. She gets *that* from your grandfather, not me!"

My chin drops, and neither Jack nor Alex will look me in the eye.

"Jack," Alex says, trying to avert the subject. "Let's help your grandma back to the house."

She slowly gets to her feet. "Thank you, gentlemen. I'm suddenly feeling like I need a wee rest."

"I suddenly feel like I need a drink," I say quietly as I follow them to the side door. Alex glances over his shoulder and smiles. My heart beats with a strange ardour. It's almost as if it's a celebration. Perhaps I've not been honest about how much I've missed him. Even when we were younger, his eyes sparkled with his infectious smile.

Alex holds the door open while Jack helps my mother up the step and into the house. "I can take it from here," I say, trying not to reveal my feelings. "I'm sure you've got things to do."

He glances at his watch. "Actually, I do have an appointment this afternoon. Can I see you later? I'll buy you that drink."

I fumble with my words, and he concedes. "I understand. You're married, and it wouldn't be appropriate."

"Who's married?" Jack asks as he comes back outside.

Alex looks at me, confused.

"Divorced," I admit reluctantly. "Things didn't work out with Jack's dad."

"Dad's been in British Columbia for twelve years," Jack adds. "You've been alone ever since."

I close my eyes, feeling embarrassed.

"I have to go," Alex says, looking pleased. "It was nice meeting you, Jack." He turns to me, and his eyes light up. "It was great seeing you again, Maya. I'll be in touch about that drink."

An internal struggle takes place within me. My head wants to decline his invitation; emphatically refuse may be a more accurate description. Somewhere deep in a tiny corner of my soul, a part of me still craves his attention and mourns his friendship. I say nothing as I watch him disappear through the garden gate.

"He's a nice guy," Jack says, breaking the silence.

"He was."

Jack raises a brow.

"He is," I correct.

"Did you know he was at every lacrosse game this season?"

"I didn't know until he told me."

22

"Oh, I forgot something." Jack bolts out of the yard, calling out to Alex.

I feel like I've just gone down the rabbit hole. I shake my head and go into the house to check on my mother. She's already sound asleep in her chair. I kiss her on the forehead. "We're leaving now. Have a good rest."

I leave through the front door and find Jack and Alex still chatting through his car window. "I thought you had to go?" I ask as I approach.

"I do. I was confirming my appointment before I headed out. I hate waiting in an empty house for a no-show."

"I don't blame you." I smile at Jack and place my hand on his back. "Grandma is already sleeping, so the rest of the day is yours. Thank you for spending time with her today."

"Of course, she's my grandma, and I love her," he says in a mature tone meant to impress Alex. I know it's not for me since I practically had to drag him here. "The guys are hanging out at Rotary Park. Can I go? If enough guys show up, they'll get a game going."

"Okay. But why can't you ever plan games at our park? Why do they always have to be on the other side of town?"

Alex chuckles. "Because the other side of town is where all the pretty girls hang out."

Jack nods his head enthusiastically, and they fist-pound each other.

"That's where you used to hang out, Maya."

Now I feel awkward again.

"I can take him if it's okay with you. My appointment is over that way, and I'm going to drive right past there."

I glance at Jack. "Are you comfortable with that?"

He laughs. "Pfft, is it okay if my mommy doesn't drop me off in front of the hot chicks? Definitely."

"Okay, okay. You don't have to hurt my feelings."

Jack skims his lips across my cheek as he walks quickly past me, likely afraid I'll change my mind. "Thanks, Mom. You're the best."

"Call me when you're ready to come home."

"I will."

Alex leans out the window and smiles before he reverses out of the driveway. I raise a hand to wave as they pull away. It's a strange feeling having time all to myself. It's been a long time since I've had friends or a hobby, so I have no idea what to do with myself. I suppose I'll do some housework since I have to work tomorrow.

All the way home, I think about Alex. He does look ruggedly handsome with that beard and the light touch of silver in his hair. It takes his charming grin and amps it up to a thousand.

As I open the front door and make my way to the family room, I remember the good times we had in my mother's backyard when we were kids. Life was simple, and together, we could take on the world. If only I could go back in time and do things differently.

I plop down on the couch and get out my phone. "Let's see what message the crow was bringing me." I scroll through the numerous results returned by my browser

search. They all say the same thing. Something is coming—
something I need to be ready for. Every nerve in my body fires
with energy, making me tingle and become acutely aware.

Hopefully, it's a sign of good things to come this time.
I need to listen to the universe and watch for signs.

Chapter Three

The sun reflects on the crystal hanging from my rear-view mirror, making sparkles dance across the dashboard of my car. Since leaving the house for work this morning, the world around me has been calling out to me as if trying to lighten my mood.

I love working with my elderly clients. Most of them are eager to regain mobility to reclaim their independence. I admire their dedication. I'm not so much enamoured with the elite sports fanatic with the uber ego whose only concern is how quickly he can return to games by putting in minimum effort because he's too busy for physio. He's the one who moans and groans and complains. Pussy.

I'm a professional, so I have to bite my tongue, but it's hard. I finish with my last client and begin to update the files. My phone rings, and I'm more than a little stunned at the name that comes up on the display.

"Alex?" I say curiously.

"Hi, Maya. I hope I haven't caught you at a bad time."

"No, I'm done for the day. I'm just updating my patient files. How did you get my number?"

"Jack."

I roll my eyes. "What a traitor," I mumble.

Alex laughs. "Don't be mad at him. I have four free tickets to a hockey game in Toronto tonight, and I wanted to take Jack and one of his friends, but I thought I should check with you."

I hate being put on the spot. "Have you been arrested for any crimes involving young boys?"

"Errr...NO."

"Are you a drunk, pedophile or junkie?"

"No, to all the above."

"Any major traffic violations or crashes?"

"Nope."

"Do you realize if anything goes wrong, you will have to deal with my mother, which will be far worse than dealing with me?"

"Actually, Maya, I was hoping you'd go with me as *my* friend."

"What?"

"Would you go with me to a hockey game?"

"Why didn't you ask me that before making me ask all those questions?"

"You didn't give me a chance, and then I was intrigued where the line of questioning was going to go," he chuckles. "How about it?"

"Are you sure Jack wants to be seen in public with his mother?"

"Well, that's why I thought he could bring a friend. Then they can pretend they don't know us."

"Until they want me to pay for food."

"Trust me, when he sees where these seats are, he won't mind sitting beside us. Can you be ready by five? I'll pick you all up at your place."

I don't know why I'm hesitating. It isn't a date if my kid and his friend are there. It's just a hockey game. "Yes, sure. Jack will love it. I'll text him right now and tell him."

"Great, I'll see you at five."

I text my son and then place my phone down beside me. Eyes burn into me from the other side of the counter. "Did you just make a date with Alex Thomas?" my coworker asks, amused.

I try to downplay it. "What? No! It's not a date."

"Right." She raises her brow.

"It's not a date," I insist. "It's just a hockey game."

"With a man."

"And my son."

She grins as she sorts through the folders to be put away. "Mmhmm."

When she steps to the side, I get a glimpse of my reflection in the window. I'm immediately shocked.

"Aren't you done for the day?" she asks as I take out my phone and look up a number.

"I am. I'm just going to see if I can get in for a haircut."

She purses her lips, trying not to smile, and places the folders back in the filing cabinet.

"You could have told me it was getting so grey."

"I think I did, and you told me you had nobody to impress."

I hold up one finger to pause her as they answer my call. "Hi, yes. It's Maya Dunn. I'm sorry for the last-minute notice, but do you have any openings for this afternoon?"

I glance up from my phone to see her shoulders rise and fall with her silent laughter. This is why I didn't bother making friends with girls in high school and still don't today.

"Great! Yes, I can be there in five minutes. I'm already in town." I gather up my things and leave without saying goodbye.

I'm greeted at the door by the salon owner. "Maya! We haven't seen you in a long time. "I follow her to the back of the room and sit in her chair.

"Far too long," I admit, looking into the mirror.

"What are we doing today?"

"Can you cover up the grey? And maybe trim the ends?"

"I can do that for you." She fusses with a bunch of things on the cart next to her, and before I know it, she's brushing colour into my hair. "Sooo. Tell me. Why the emergency appointment?"

I hesitate, and she breaks into a wide, toothy smile. "Oh! You've got a date, don't you?"

"No, it's not a date."

She stops applying the colour and cocks her head to the side.

I stare at her in the mirror in front of me. "It's a hockey game with an old friend. My kid and one of his friends are coming with us."

She piles the saturated hair on the top of my head. "Is this old friend a man?"

"Yes."

"Then it's a date."

"I give up. It's a date."

"Although," she continues. "I shouldn't have said if it's a man, it's a date. These days, it could have been another woman and be a date." She sets the timer and places it on the table.

"This is true."

"I wouldn't judge you if this was the case. I didn't think it was your thing."

"Nope. I prefer men."

"A lot of people these days don't limit themselves to one or the other. They love who they love. Man, Woman...Unlabeled."

My eyes widen. "Why are we having this conversation right now?" My phone rings, and I've never been happier about an interruption. She pats me on the shoulder.

"I'll be back when the timer goes off."

I nod as I answer. "Hey, Jack."

"Tyler's mom wants to know how much she owes us for the ticket."

"Alex said they were free, so nothing. Just make sure he has money with him for food and drinks."

With the phone still to his ear, he yells my answer back to Tyler through the online game. The roar pierces my brain. "Did you have to yell in my ear?"

"Sorry, Mom. I'm just excited."

"It's okay. Listen, Alex wants to be on our way at five. That means we're ready to go and not the usual *turn the video game off at five and wander to the shower*. Tell Tyler to be at our place no later than four-thirty. We'll drop him off at home after the game."

"Got it. What time will you be home?"

"In about an hour. I've got to go. Your aunt is calling." That's a shock. I connect her call. "Hi, June."

"Hey, Maya. I got your message. What's going on?"

"Mom's not herself lately. I'm a little worried."

"What do you mean?"

"She sleeps a lot and barely eats."

"Well, she is getting older."

"I don't know. Something seems *off* to me."

"I see. Your so-called *spidey sense* is tingling."

I know she's ridiculing me, and my body tenses. "Sort of. Don't you ever get feelings about things?"

"Not like you."

I don't believe I'm the only one. "Anyway...have you talked to your brother lately?"

"No, I never hear from him. He's busy doing whatever it is he does."

"I know everybody's busy, June. Do you think you guys could spend a little more time with Mom? She's lonely and misses you. Call her once a week to check in and say hello. She's not going to be around forever." I can't believe I just put that out into the universe.

"Sure, Maya. I'll try."

"Could you call Brian for me, please? He's not answering my texts."

"Will do. I've got to run. The girls have gymnastics."

"Tell them I love them, and I hope to see them soon." My shoulders fall when I realize she's already hung up. "I'll try," I mumble. "That means I'll tell you what you want to hear but do nothing."

"Are you talking to yourself?" the stylist asks, returning to the room.

"Pretty much."

"I do that all the time. People think I'm crazy."

I bite my tongue and scroll through my social media notifications.

I chuckle at one of the requests.

"Oh," she says, looking over my shoulder. "Alex Thomas sent you a friend request." She pauses and then gasps. "Is he the old friend you're going out with tonight?"

"Really? You're reading my phone over my shoulder?"

"I knew it. It is!" she squeals. "He is so handsome. A friend of mine listed her house with him, and she was crushing on him big time."

I try to get a few words in, but she continues to ramble.

"Don't you worry. When you leave here, you'll feel like a new woman."

I stare into the mirror. "Good because the old woman looks tired, boring, and close to adopting her first of many cats. Let's do this."

It took longer than an hour, but I leave the salon feeling more beautiful than I have in a long time. The closer I get to home, the more butterflies I get about seeing Alex tonight. It's a ridiculous response, and I try to reason with myself. I hate that he's stirred up these emotions in me. The hormones just need to calm the fuck down.

"Jack!" I holler as I open the door. "Are you ready?" I can hear him and Tyler in his room playing a video game.

I climb the stairs and get the strangest feeling that I'm not alone. I pause midway and lean over the railing to peruse the first floor. No intruders, no shadows...nothing. I shrug. "Not tonight, third eye. I'm shutting you off so I can enjoy my evening without making people think I'm crazy."

I knock once before I open the door to find them sitting cross-legged on the floor at the end of the bed with controllers in hand and headsets on. "Jack!"

He looks over his left shoulder and slides a headphone off one of his ears. "Hey, mom."

"Are you ready?"

His brow furrows. "It's a hockey game. How do we need to be any more ready than we are now?"

I supposed he has a point. "Don't get wrapped up in a game you can't quit. Alex will be here soon."

His player dies, and Tyler cheers. Jack gives me a frustrated look. "Thanks, Mom."

"It's only a game, Jack." I hurry down the hallway and throw open my cupboard door. I'm unsure why I'm having difficulty picking an outfit. I change several times before I'm happy with my choice. I finish putting on mascara when the

34

doorbell rings. Two pairs of thunderous footsteps bound down the stairs.

"Mom! Alex is here!"

"Coming!" I take a deep breath and look at myself one last time in the mirror. "Be rational, Maya," I say aloud as I start down the stairs. "There can never be anything between you and Alex."

"Whoa!" Jack exclaims as I come into view.

"What's the matter?" I ask, concerned. "Is there something wrong with what I'm wearing? I can change!"

Alex beams with delight. "There's nothing wrong with what you're wearing. You look beautiful."

"Are you wearing makeup?" Jack asks, looking astonished as I reach the bottom of the stairs.

Alex holds open the front door. "I love your hair. It suits you."

"Thank you," I say as I pass. "It feels pretty."

"What's different about your hair?" Jack asks, confused, as he walks to the car.

"Seriously?" I ask, raising a brow. "You can spot a spy camouflaged in the bushes in your video game, but you didn't notice that I got my hair cut and coloured?"

Jack looks at Alex, confused.

"You need to pay attention to those things, buddy. They're important to girls. They expect you to notice."

"Yes, we do," I say as I get into the front seat of Alex's SUV.

Everyone gets in, and Alex starts driving. "Girls also stop talking to you for no apparent reason. You may never know what you did."

I shoot a death glare in Alex's direction. "Well, if they stop talking to you, it's for a good reason, and you must know what you did."

"What are they talking about?" Tyler asks Jack.

He replies with a shrug.

Alex looks in the mirror at the boys. "Girls also hold grudges *forever*."

I nod my head enthusiastically in agreement.

Alex grins, and it irks me. The lights in the city are beautiful. As we park and walk toward the arena, I let it go. At least for tonight.

"There are many people here tonight," Alex says to the boys after we enter the building. "If we get separated, go to gate one hundred and ten and wait there. We'll meet you there with your tickets."

The lack of response concerns me. "Did you hear that, boys?"

"Yes," Tyler says, looking overwhelmed at the crowd moving around us.

"What gate do you need to meet us at if you get separated?"

"One hundred and Ten," the boys answer in unison.

"We have seat service," Alex advises. "So don't stop for snacks out here."

I raise a brow. "Isn't it more expensive to order it that way?"

"Don't worry, Maya. Let them enjoy the grand experience."

I'm glad I opted for comfortable shoes instead of fancy boots. It feels like we walk the entire circumference of the arena before we get to our gate.

"Holy cow, I hope there aren't too many stairs to climb. I'm exhausted."

Alex smirks. "There aren't any stairs to climb."

We follow him to the seats, and Alex's chest puffs out with pride as the boys explode into excitement.

"These are the seats?" Jack asks, surprised.

"These are the seats," Alex confirms.

"Mom, can you believe this? We're sitting right behind the player's bench."

"Yes, I see." I turn to Alex with an anxious expression. "Does this mean we'll be on camera the entire game?"

He chuckles. "Yup."

I frown. "Maybe I'll go watch from the bar."

"Sit," he says as he takes his seat beside Jack. "You shouldn't deny the world the opportunity to see how lovely you look tonight."

The world? Slight apprehension turns into a vast, uncomfortable bout of nerves, but I don't want to miss out on watching my son enjoy this. It's not likely something I'd ever be able to do for him again.

I'm on high alert when the game starts, knowing that my every movement could be visible in the background on the television broadcast. I'm not as worried about everyone in town seeing me here with Alex as I am about doing something that will come back to embarrass him…or my son. My hair looks pretty damn awesome, in any case.

"Can we order something to eat?" Jack asks, leaning around Alex.

"As long as you can afford it."

Alex reaches for his wallet. "Start filling in the order. You need a credit card to pay."

"I can get mine out."

"It's okay," Alex assures me. "The boys can pay me later."

"I'm sure they'll forget to do that."

"Then it becomes a business expense. Tell me, have you ever thought about selling your home?"

I smile. Looking into his chestnut-coloured eyes, I forget for the time being why I've been avoiding him for nearly seventeen years.

"I'll take a beer," Alex says to Jack.

"What about you, Mom?"

"Oh, no!" Alex says, stopping him. "Your mother cannot have a beer at a hockey game."

"Why not? Does she get drunk and obnoxious?"

I scowl. "Have either of you ever seen me drunk and obnoxious?"

"Not me," Alex says as he looks at Jack. "How about you?"

"I don't think I've ever seen her drink."

"I'll have popcorn," I say, interrupting their conversation.

"Is she allowed popcorn?" Jack asks.

Alex nods. "Sure, I suppose she could do minimal damage with popcorn."

Jack's brow creases with curiosity, and I ignore him when I see him lean back to look at me behind Alex.

It doesn't take long for the food to be delivered to our seats. Alex carefully places his beer away from me. "You're funny," I say sarcastically.

"We don't need another incident," he says, chuckling.

I enjoy watching the boys as they are entirely immersed in the game. I'm glad it's almost over because constantly thinking about what I'm doing and what viewers see is exhausting.

The score is tied, and the crowd is buzzing with excitement. You can feel the tension around us. As our team advances toward the net and scores, I get caught up in the thrill of the moment, and as I jump to my feet, I throw my hands in the air, scattering popcorn all over the people around me.

Horrified, I apologize profusely. Everyone brushes kernels off themselves while giving me annoyed looks. Alex and the kids are trying hard to hide their laughter.

"Now you know what happened to the beer last time she drank at a game," I hear Alex say quietly to Jack.

My worst nightmare comes true as I sit back in my seat to watch the rest of the game, and every screen around the arena is a replay of the goal, followed by a close-up shot of my popcorn mishap. The entire arena erupts in laughter, and I do my best to keep my composure. I wave at the camera as they pan over to a live shot of us. I can see from the big screen close-up that the poor woman behind me still has popcorn in her hair.

"I think I'm going to die," I say quietly to Alex when the camera returns to game coverage. He reaches over and holds my hand. "You're fine. Have fun. You've given your boy memories he'll keep with him for the rest of his life."

I'm horrified, so I'm not sure if it's a coping mechanism or a nervous reaction, but I begin to laugh. I hold my hand over my mouth, trying to conceal it, but I can't stop. Alex chuckles and squeezes my hand tighter.

We wait for the arena to empty halfway before getting to our feet. Alex keeps his hand on my back as we manoeuvre through the crowds to the parking garage. The boys don't stop talking the entire drive home. I glance over my shoulder and smile.

I focus my attention on Alex. "Thank you. I think they had a good time."

"It was my pleasure. How about you? Did you have a good time?"

"I did. Well, until the popcorn incident."

"Look on the bright side. Now you're a celebrity." He breaks into a wide smile.

I'm thankful for a quieter ride after we drop Tyler off until Jack's phone rings. "We're almost home. I'll be online in ten minutes. Dude! My mom's boyfriend took us to a hockey game tonight."

My eyes open wide, and I look apologetically at Alex. He smiles and whispers, "Just let it go."

"We had seats right behind the team bench. We could hear the players swearing and everything! Tyler went too," Jack continues.

"I'll set it straight later," I promise.

"Well, technically, I am a boy, and we are friends," Alex points out.

I grimace. "Are we in high school again?"

"Thank you. That was the best night ever," Jack yells as he jumps out of the car before we've even stopped.

"I'm glad you enjoyed it."

"Jack," I shout, trying to slow him down. I turn to Alex and give him an apologetic look. "I'm sorry."

"Don't apologize. He said thank you, and while you went for a bathroom break, they paid me for their snacks."

"WOW! I did not see that happening."

He gets out of the car and walks with me toward the house. When we reach the door, I stop and turn to face him like a nervous teenager. "Do you want to come in for a coffee?"

"I have a very early open house tomorrow. Another time?"

I smile. "I'd like that. Thank you again. Now that lacrosse is over, he's always on that damn video game."

"Let him be a kid just a little bit longer. Adulting is hard."

I know he's right, so I nod. "Good night."

Alex moves closer, and my heart begins to beat faster, sending a surge of excitement through me. I close my eyes, preparing for a kiss, as he lifts his hand toward my face. His hand brushes through my hair, but his lips don't find mine. I flutter open my eyes to see what's going on.

Alex is watching me, amused. "You have popcorn in your hair." He smirks as he brushes his hand through my hair again, knocking the popcorn onto the ground.

"Oh." I lower my eyes, feeling embarrassed.

Alex brushes a sweet kiss on my cheek. "Goodnight, Maya. Thanks for the wonderful night."

Words get stuck in my throat, so I wave as he gets into his car and drives away. After all these years, I'm standing here feeling off-balance and emotional. Maybe even excited. I can't put a name to it, but the feelings I'm experiencing now scare me more than when our innocent childhood friendship blossomed into love. I'm definitely going to overthink it.

Chapter Four

I arrive at work the following day tired from a long night of restless sleep. As I open the door, a crow zooms past my head, making me jump. Its loud caw aggravates me. "Get out of here, you noisy bird. I don't have any time for your nonsense today."

We must be fully booked because all the curtains are drawn at the therapy stations. I look around as I go to the room where the staff leave their personal belongings. Oddly, there's no one around. If we're this busy, there are usually therapists running around frantically.

I walk past a half-drawn curtain, and suddenly, I'm pelted with popcorn. Startled, I stop in my tracks and look around me as the jokesters fail to hide their snickering.

"Very funny." I shake popcorn off me and become aware of the eyes peeking out from behind the curtains. I shake my head and carry on.

When I return to the room, one of the girls is sweeping popcorn into a dustpan, and everyone else is attending to business as usual. Everyone avoids eye contact with me. Apparently, we're just going to pretend it didn't happen.

My first few clients are eager to tell me they saw me on television. I try to maintain my sense of humour. This is going to be the longest day ever. I grab a folder off the pile of charts they've left for me to review and pull back the curtain in the first treatment room.

My eyes open wide. "Mason!"

"Hi, Maya. What's with the popcorn all over the floor?"

"I take it you didn't watch the hockey game last night?"

"No, I didn't. I'm way behind on chores. I was trying to get the winter wheat planted and praying it's not too late in the season."

"Well, you may be the only person in town who didn't watch it." I flip open the folder and quickly skim the details, hoping to change the subject. "What happened? Why are you here?"

"I tweaked something trying to repair the south fence."

"Are you still living on the farm in Grey County?"

"I am. It will always be home, but it's gruelling work these days."

"It's beautiful up there."

"Stop in and say hello next time you're out that way."

"I will. Now, let's see what's going on. Is it your back?" I look at the copy of the X-ray in the file.

"No, the doctor says it's my neck."

I put down the chart and begin my assessment. "Does this hurt?"

He cringes as he answers. "Quite a bit."

"There's severe inflammation here. Did the doctor prescribe something for that?"

"Yup. I just started taking them, and he said it may take some time to get into my system and start to work."

"What exactly were you doing when you felt the pain?"

"Trying to hold the top fence board with my shoulder while I fastened it to the post."

"You were repairing the fence alone?"

"There's only me out there. My dad can't tend to things like that anymore."

"Sorry to hear that. You know, you're no spring chicken yourself anymore."

He scowls at me, and I grin.

"Maya," he says, concerned. "I can't afford to be out of commission for long, and I don't have medical insurance. I'm paying for these appointments out of my savings."

"I nod. I'll work out a plan for most of the stretches and strengthening exercises so you can do those at home."

"I'm not afraid of hard work."

"I know you're not." I walk with him to the front desk. "We'll do a quick weekly follow-up to monitor the progress and hold off on additional treatments for now to keep the bill to a minimum. If we need to do ultrasound treatments or anything else, we'll work something out."

"I appreciate it, Maya. Thank you."

"You betcha." The office manager hands me a slip of paper. "She's scheduled another appointment for the end of the week."

"Wow, she's efficient. How did she know you wanted to see me again."

The office manager smiles. "I'm psychic."

"Not true," I assure him. "Sound travels in here. She can hear everything being said in that exam room."

I walk him to the door. "We'll start with a massage and see if we can't loosen up some of this stiffness. By then, I'll have a plan for the homework."

He grimaces as he puts on his jacket. I frown as if I feel his pain. I wish I could wave a magic wand and make it go away, but I know it will take time. "Mason, take it easy if you can. The muscles need to rest before everything can start to heal. Okay?"

He nods as he folds his appointment papers and stuffs them into the inside pocket of his jacket. I reach for the door as it's flung open and nearly stumble outside. I curse as a pair of strong arms catch me.

"Whoa, are you okay?" Alex asks as he returns me to my feet.

"I think so."

His face lights up. "Mason Davis! Long time no see. How are you, buddy?" He looks around the room. "I guess you're not okay if you're here to see Maya."

"Just a pinched nerve in my neck."

"I hope you got that the fun way."

I scowl at him.

"I wish," Mason chuckles. "Unfortunately, it's the south fence for the win."

"Sorry to hear that."

46

"Are you here for treatment?" Mason asks.

My face turns red.

"No. I just came to see if I could talk Maya into taking a break."

Mason looks at me and then at Alex and raises a brow. "Well, I'll get on my way. If I don't get back, my dad will try and do the chores on his own."

Alex pats him on the back. "Take care. It was great seeing you again."

Alex grins at me. I feel awkward and uncomfortable. Maybe a little bit excited. "How about it? Do you have time to grab a coffee with me?"

"Yes, she does!" The office manager says. "Her next client isn't until one o'clock."

"That's great. Grab your jacket."

I glance at the office manager as I walk past her to grab my purse. "He's cute." She mouths.

My face turns red again.

Alex takes my jacket out of my hands and holds it for me to put on. When he sweeps his hand across my neck to straighten the collar, every nerve in my body fires up and comes alive as if I were a spark plug ignited by his touch. I'm thankful for the cool breeze as it calms my reaction when we step out onto the street. "There's a wonderful café a few doors down. We could have a quick lunch."

"I know it well. The Songbird Cafe is one of my favourite places to take clients. They have a great lunch."

"I love it. They have the best soup in town." As we walk, his hand brushes against mine, and if it wasn't such a brief walk, I'm sure he would have held it.

Always the perfect gentleman, he holds the door open for me and places his hand on the small of my back when the waitress ushers us to a table by the window.

"I'm surprised they aren't packed in here," I say, looking around the room.

"It will be in about ten minutes," the waitress says as she places menus in front of us.

"I know what I want," I say as I hand her back the menu. "I'd like the *soup of the day*."

"You don't want to know what it is first?" Alex asks, amused.

"Nope. It doesn't matter. I like them all."

He passes his menu to the waitress and grins. "Make it two soups."

I raise my brow. "You're only having soup?"

"Yes, why?"

"I remember you having a much bigger appetite."

"I was a teenage boy back then. I don't need that many calories anymore. Unless I'm going to the gym."

Soup bowls are placed before us, and I inhale the rich smell. "Oh, this is the best garden vegetable I have ever had."

"It's hot," the waitress warns.

Alex blows on the spoonful he's about to put in his mouth. I watch, anticipating his reaction.

His eyes open wide as he swallows. "Hot," he confirms. "Really hot." He chugs his water. "You didn't tell me it was spicy. I thought she meant the temperature."

I smile and then laugh. "They use peppers they grow themselves. All the vegetables they serve come from a garden at the back of the building or from local farmers."

He dabs the sweat from his forehead with the back of his hand. I frown. "I'm sorry. I should have warned you. Order something else."

"I'm good. I wasn't expecting it."

I butter a roll and pass it to him. "The bread helps."

"You enjoyed that, didn't you?"

"A little bit." Alex never gave in to a challenge, so he took on that bowl of soup like a champ. I giggle when he asks the waitress for another basket of rolls.

"Seeing Mason was quite a surprise."

"It was. I didn't know he was coming in."

"How bad is his injury?"

"It's a pinched nerve and inflammation. It's easy to treat, but he needs to rest the muscles, and I don't think he will do that."

"No? Why's that?"

"He was saying his dad can't help much around the farm anymore, so it's up to him to do all the repairs and chores himself. He hurt himself lifting fence boards on his own."

"That's ridiculous. I'll call Ben and Jake, and maybe we can go up and help."

I smile. "That would be nice of you. They were younger than us, right?"

"Yes, they used to hang out with an older cousin I played lacrosse with."

"Right! The McCarthy clan. I remember now. They were always tagging along."

"Now they come in handy when I find myself listing a home that's a little tired and needing some rejuvenation."

"I heard Jake sells pieces he's salvaged and upcycled."

Alex peruses the bill and then leaves cash on the table. "He does. And Ben is an expert in historical restoration. He's handled almost all the restoration work downtown. They wouldn't mind spending an afternoon helping Mason out."

"I love our community. When somebody needs help, everyone is there for them." I look at my watch. "Oh shoot. I can't believe it's almost one o'clock already."

Alex looks at his phone. "Wow, time went fast."

As I push back my chair to get to my feet, Alex reaches out for my hand. I pause.

"Maya, it's great spending time with you again. You haven't changed at all."

"Thank you for lunch. I hope you still want to be friends later tonight when that soup comes back to haunt you."

His expression is suddenly filled with dread as he holds open the door. "I'll walk you back."

I try to make him forget about it on the short walk back to the clinic. "Jack and Tyler are still raving about the great seats. Thank you again."

"My pleasure. I'm glad it worked out. I always get tickets and turn them down because I don't have anyone to go with." He holds open the clinic door.

I walk past the front desk with Alex right behind me. The room is calm, and it makes me feel uneasy. It only takes a second before I realize what we're walking into. I try to warn Alex, but we're hit with a torrent of popcorn before I can speak a single word. Instinctively, I protect my face until the storm fades and they run out of ammunition. Laughter echoes through the clinic. I peek through my hands and then drop them to my side as I look around the room. Alex is doing his best not to laugh.

"It will take you all afternoon to clean up this mess." I holler.

"It was worth it!" the office manager yells from behind one of the exam room curtains.

I frown as I turn toward Alex. "They're never going to let it go."

Alex chuckles and picks popcorn out of my hair as the room springs to life and everyone returns to work. The office manager drags out the industrial vacuum. I shake my head, disapproving of the effort required for a few laughs.

"Well, I should let you get back to work. I'm not sure if I should thank you for lunch since you tried to kill me."

I try not to smile. "You're very dramatic for a real estate agent."

"I am?"

"Yes, you should have gone into theatre."

"I'll keep that in mind if selling houses doesn't pan out."

I open the door, and he steps out. Then he pauses and turns. "Can I call you later?"

A million thoughts about all the opportunities and missed moments in the past seventeen years run through my mind. "Sure."

He smirks as I close the door on his victorious expression. I close my eyes. What did I do? I shake my head, trying to reset my thoughts so I can return to work.

Chapter Five

I hate taking evening clients. It makes it feel like the day is never going to end. When I finally get home, I'm too tired to put much thought into dinner, so I opt for a quick snack and then tidy the kitchen. I'm intrigued when there's a knock on the door. I'm not expecting anyone. "Just a minute," I holler, drying my hands on a tea towel as I walk toward the front door.

I'm shocked to find Alex standing there as the door swings open. "Alex! What are you doing here? You said you were going to call."

"I did? I thought I said I'd stop in."

"No, you asked if you could call."

He raises his brow and leans to look around the partially opened door. "Well, I'm here now. Can I come in?"

I look down at the worn-out pyjama pants I'm wearing and feel embarrassed. "I suppose so." I reluctantly loosen my grip on the edge of the door.

"Great! I hope I'm not interrupting anything."

"I was just washing the dinner dishes."

He follows me into the kitchen. "Perfect timing then."

"For what?"

He holds up a paper bag. "I brought dessert. I had a craving for something sweet, so I stopped at the bakeshop downtown because they make the best cinnamon rolls."

I open the cupboard and get down two plates as he opens the bag.

"Look at the size of this thing. It's enough for four people!"

I cringe. "That is a LOT of calories right there."

"You don't look like you need to watch your weight. You're as beautiful as you were in high school."

I feel my face start to warm, and I hand him a knife to distract him from noticing. He moves half the monstrous cinnamon roll to the plate in front of me. My teeth hurt just looking at it. I pick it up and glance over at him. "Well...thanks for the diabetes." The first mouthful is rich and decadent. I savour every moment of it. "Okay, this is good."

"Right?" Alex licks the icing off his fingers.

I concede after the second bite. "I can't eat any more of this right now. I'm sure Jack will finish it for me later."

"Where is Jack?" Alex shoves his last bite into his mouth.

"At a friend's house. He'll be home soon."

"Would you like to go to the movies or something in town?"

I glance down at my attire and wrinkle my nose. "I can't see me getting dressed again."

Disappointment darkens his eyes.

"We could just move to the living room and watch a movie online?"

His expression lightens. "Have you got any wine?"

I laugh. "Is that a serious question?" I grab two glasses and a bottle from the cabinet.

"Where's your corkscrew?" He asks, getting to his feet and trying to be helpful.

"Pfft." I chuckle and unscrew the lid. "Like I'm a connoisseur. If you like fancy expensive wine, you're at the wrong place."

He laughs. "I'm perfectly okay with your choice."

After a single glass of wine, we've travelled back in time twenty years, sitting on the couch disagreeing on what shows to watch and arguing over the best Marvel character. An hour later, we're still undecided, so I turn off the T.V. Alex becomes silent and stares at me with a ghost of a smile.

I put my wine down and sit back. "Why are you here, Alex? And don't tell me it's because you couldn't eat the cinnamon roll by yourself. I've seen you muck through more food than that in one sitting."

His shoulders tense. "For seventeen years, I didn't know what happened between us. I need to know."

"You don't know?" I say, astonished.

"No, Maya. I still have no idea. Our last night together was the most amazing night of my life. And then you stopped taking my calls and wouldn't come to the door when I came to the house. I tried for months, and then I heard that you were marrying Kevin, and shortly afterwards, I heard you were having a baby."

My stomach twists in knots. "I'm surprised that you cared."

"How could you say that? Of course, I cared. I was crushed."

"Every time I saw you, you were with that girl."

Alex's brow creases. "Girl?"

"The one with the red hair and big boobs."

"Hilary? She was in one of my classes. We were working on a project together."

"Was the class sex education, by any chance? Because I saw it with my own eyes."

"You saw what? Nothing was going on."

"I saw you kissing her."

"I don't know what you saw, Maya, but that never happened. So, you saw me with another girl and assumed the worst? Do you honestly think I would do that to you?"

I feel regret. "When you say it aloud, I sound like a dick."

The door swings open, and Jack barrels in, dropping his heavy bag in the hallway. "Mom?" he hollers.

Alex exhales and reaches for my hand. I feel my body stiffen as I rapidly blink, hoping to hide the tears beginning to well up in my eyes.

"We're in here!" I answer.

Alex frowns as I get to my feet. "How was your day?"

"It was okay. No homework tonight, so that's always a bonus." He pauses as he enters the room and sees Alex. "Hey."

"Hey, how's it going?" He gets to his feet and taps knuckles with him.

"Good." He looks at Alex and then at me. "I'm going to play online for a little while."

"Not too late."

"Yes, ma'am," he groans as he makes his way upstairs.

There's an awkward silence between Alex and me. He rakes his fingers through his hair. "Okay, let's just table this conversation for now. We were young. I'm here tonight because having you back in my life has made me happier than I've been for a very long time. There's been something missing since you left."

I fidget uncomfortably. "You know I'm overthinking this."

Alex smiles. "Yes, I know. Let's try to let the past stay in the past. You're single, so am I... we enjoy each other's company. Let's see where it goes."

I try to stall my brain. It seems reasonable. I'd be lying if I said that I haven't felt happier lately as well.

I sit down and pick up the remote. "I'm picking the movie."

Alex exhales a sigh of relief. "Okay. I'll pick next time."

I fill our wine glasses. "We'll see. I wouldn't get your hopes up."

"Not much has changed."

I grin.

"How's your mom?"

I pause. "You know, I didn't hear from her today. I was going to call her after I finished the dishes."

"Does she normally call every day?"

"Not always, but it's never more than two days." Concern washes over me as I realize she didn't call me yesterday either.

"Go ahead and call her. I don't mind."

I glance at my phone. "It's too late. I'm sure she's sleeping. I'll call her in the morning on my way to work."

Alex leans back and gets comfortable, and I follow suit. It feels like no time has passed since we were teenagers. It's a liberating feeling. For too long in my adult life, I've struggled with issues that make it hard to trust or lean on others for support.

Partly because I grew up with siblings who only cared about themselves and partly because those I thought would always have my back let me down when I was most vulnerable. Alex fell in the latter category.

He reaches for my hand and tangles our fingers together. I clear my mind of self-sabotage and overthinking. I don't want to fuck this up again.

"I think I've seen that movie a hundred times, and it still makes me laugh." I stretch and yawn as the movie ends.

Alex reaches for the remote and turns off the television. "I better get going. It's late."

I get to my feet and walk him to the door. "Thanks for hanging out with me tonight."

He pauses as if trying to memorize every inch of my face. My heart races as I wonder if this is the moment that he brings his lips to mine.

"I was wondering."

"What?" I ask softly, trying to hide the anticipation I'm feeling.

"There's a sales awards dinner for my real estate firm on the weekend. Would you go with me? I mean, they're really long and boring."

I furrow my brow. "Funny, I thought you'd be better at selling things than that."

He grins. "You'd think. On a positive note, the food is always decent, and there's a bar."

"Okay, now you've got my attention. What's the dress code?"

"Dress to impress but not black tie."

"And you'd be my date?"

"Yes, but I'm not sure that's a selling point either."

I watch the rise and fall of his heavily muscled chest. "I'm in."

A look of relief washes over him. "I'll text you the details."

I lean in. I want his mouth on me more than anything I've ever wanted before.

He steps back, putting a frustrating distance between us. "I'll call you tomorrow."

I close the door behind him and lean against it, resisting the urge to run after him and beg him to stay.

My mind churns in a million directions. I turn off the lights and get into bed, but sleep eludes me. I think...and overthink. I wonder why now? Alex said he thinks the time is finally right for us. How does he know for sure?

My life, at times, feels like an endless game of variables. Maybe the crow means good things are to come, or perhaps it means something is going to change. It could be both. I wish for once the universe would send me a direct message instead of sending me signs.

I toss and turn several times before throwing off the blankets and getting out of bed.

I dig through the closet for an old scrapbook and then sit in the corner chair, thumbing through memories. The last entry is a picture of Alex and me at the fall fair. It was an exciting night of carnival rides and games. It's funny how that seems like a romantic date when you're only seventeen. Especially when your best friend confesses his love. That night, I gave myself to him completely, and everything changed.

Hours later, I place the book on the floor and climb back into bed. I lay awake in the dark thinking about the last night I spent with Alex and the torturous days that followed. Visions and intuitive feelings haunted me back then, dragging me down a dark path and away from him. It was no one's fault but my own. It was all me. Alex's voice echoes in my mind as my eyes grow heavy and I drift into sleep. *Leave the past in the past and look forward.*

Chapter Six

Everything I see today reminds me of Alex. I'm looking forward to accompanying him to his awards dinner. There are no signs or messages from the universe today—just a warm, sunny morning with cheerful birds and hot coffee.

I called my mom several times during the morning when I had time between patients, but she isn't answering. Suddenly, my peaceful morning turns grey, and the overwhelming feeling of impending doom haunts me. I've been sensitive to universal vibrations since I was a child. I learned not to ignore such a strong feeling as an adult.

I get in my car and drive there on my lunch break to ensure everything is okay.

A crow sits on the corner fence as I turn onto her street. Then another and another until there are several in a row. I feel panic wash over me. I'm sure I'll be scolded or ridiculed for my concern and accused of overthinking because that's how they explain intuitive feelings they don't understand. I'll take the chance. Something doesn't feel right. Everything looks normal outside, so I knock and then let myself in.

I call out for her as I walk through the rooms on the main floor. I try to convince myself she's out shopping or at an appointment to calm my unease as I slowly walk toward the bedroom door and push it open. Terror runs through my veins when I see her crumpled body on the floor. I scream her name and rush to her, unsure of what to do when I get there.

I call her, trying to wake her and dial my phone for emergency assistance.

"Hurry, please!" I beg before disconnecting the call. Suddenly, her eyes open and flutter.

"Maya?" she says in a strained, muted voice.

"I'm here, Mom. Help is on the way. What happened? Did you faint? Did you fall?"

Her eyes flutter and then close again. A terrifying moment follows until I confirm she's still breathing. Slow and shallow, but she's still taking breaths. I can hear the sirens approaching, so I leave her to greet them at the door.

"I don't know what happened," I say desperately as I step outside. "I came to check on her and found her on the floor."

"Is she conscious?" a tall, lanky man asks as he pushes the gurney toward the house.

"She opened her eyes and said my name, but that's all. She mentioned the other day that she hadn't had much appetite. Maybe she's got a bug, or her blood sugar is low."

The loud clatter of metal makes me grimace as they force the gurney through the door. I follow, giving directions to her room as they go down the hall. Without hesitation, they push furniture out of the way to make room and kneel beside her on the floor to check her vitals and assess the situation.

"We're going to roll her onto her back slowly," the second paramedic says, looking up at me. They recheck her. "I don't see any bumps, bruises or visible signs of breaks that we would look for in a fall scenario," the taller man says as they bundle her up and lift her onto the gurney. "Her blood pressure is low but stable, so we'll get her to the hospital and find out what's going on."

I nod. A loud voice hollers my name as the front door slams shut. "MAYA!" He steps out of the way to allow the paramedic to pass, but his eyes never leave mine.

"Alex, what are you doing here?" I ask as I reach him.

"I was driving past and saw the ambulance outside. What happened? Is she okay?" He places his hands on my arms, and I welcome the familiar, calming touch.

"I don't know. I found her unconscious on the floor in her bedroom."

He follows me out of the house and locks the door behind him.

I anxiously watch as they load her into the ambulance and get the attention of one of the paramedics. "Can I go with her?"

"I'm afraid not. You can meet her there."

"What if she wakes up? She'll be scared and confused."

"We'll take good care of her." The door closes, leaving me unsettled. I brush my hand across my forehead and pause.

"I'll drive you there," Alex says, concerned.

"No. No, I'm okay."

"Maya," he says in a commanding voice. "You're upset, and there's not a chance in hell I'm letting you get behind the wheel of a vehicle. Don't argue with me."

I suddenly feel weak and lightheaded, and I know I'm likely on the verge of a panic attack. "Okay." I concede with a nod.

He looks at me suspiciously as I follow him to his car. "Are you okay?"

"Not really."

"Obviously. I was expecting more of an argument."

I shrug. The only thing on my mind is my mother. He follows the ambulance to the hospital, and it comforts me that she's still in my sight.

"It's a good sign," he says as he concentrates on driving.

"What is?"

"That they only had their lights on. If she was in distress or danger, the siren would have been blaring, and they would have driven Mach one all the way here."

I suppose he's right, but it fails to comfort me as we pull into the parking lot. A crow swoops in and lands on the hood of his SUV the minute we come to a complete stop. It stares at me with menacing eyes.

Alex gets out of the vehicle and shoes it away. "That's a little ominous," he says as he opens my door.

As I walk toward the hospital on high alert, my eyes dart in every direction. "More than a little ominous," I agree.

Alex follows me to the nurse's station in the emergency room and stands by my side while I wait to find out where she is.

"Are you here with the woman who came in by ambulance?" the triage nurse whispers with her hand over the phone speaker.

"Yes," Alex answers for me.

"Follow the blue line around the corner. She's in the hallway to the right until we have a vacant room for her."

Alex guides me with his hand on the small of my back. I'm glad he's here because I'm still in a fog. When we find her, she's partially sitting up and drinking from a straw while the paramedic holds the cup.

"She was thirsty," he says as we approach.

It's a relief to see her awake and alert.

"Maya? What are you doing here?"

"I dropped in to check on you, and it looks like it's a good thing I did."

"I don't remember what happened. I was going to make some breakfast, and that's all I know. I feel fine now, so there's no need to trouble anybody. Could you drive me back home?"

I glance at Alex, who looks as stunned as I feel. "Ummm, that's a big NO. You need to find out what happened and why you've not been feeling well lately."

She scowls. "I just hate to be such a bother." She can tell by my unwavering expression that I'm not giving in, so she turns to Alex with a look of desperation. "Please, dear."

Alex raises a brow, amused that she thinks he has any say in the matter. "Sorry, Gladys, you should listen to your daughter. She's right. You need to find out what's going on."

"Excuse me," an orderly says as he nudges his way past and unlocks the wheels on the gurney. "We're going to take her for some x-rays and a scan."

As he pushes her down the hallway and out of sight, a woman wearing a cardigan three sizes too big approaches. "Are you family?"

"Yes, I'm her daughter."

"Here's her health card. She'll be in three zero seven."

I look around for numbers on the bed, then stare at her, confused.

"Not here in the emergency department," she explains. "That's her room number. Dr. Murray is in doing rounds today, so we called him. He's admitted her, and he'll be around to see her later."

"I don't know who that is. Her family doctor is Barry Wilton."

"Dr. Murray is her oncologist." She pulls the sweater around her as she walks away.

An instant shot of terror pulses through my veins. Alex reaches over and grasps my hand. I'm frozen where I am.

"Maya," he says sympathetically.

"Did she just say, oncologist?"

He squeezes my hand firmly as he confirms. "Yes."

"Her oncologist is on file. As in, she's seen him previously, and she knows she has cancer?"

"It appears so. I'm so sorry."

I take my phone out of my pocket. "I'll phone work and cancel all my afternoon appointments."

"What about Jack?"

"I don't want to call him at school and upset him. I'll wait until he gets home to talk to him."

"Okay, but I'm worried about *you,* so I'll stay."

"You don't have to do that. I'll go to the room and wait to meet Dr. Murray."

"I've got nothing booked this afternoon. I'm not asking for permission."

I would normally defy the absolute control in his voice, but I'm overwhelmed with emotion and worry. "Thank you."

The corner of his lip curls into a subtle victory grin. "You're welcome."

The nurse with the oversized sweater turns the corner with a stack of folded blankets. "The room upstairs is ready, so you can wait for your mom up there."

I nod and walk the long, sterile hallway to the foyer. When we step into the elevator, I'm hit with a faint trace of smoke. "Do you smell that?"

"I do."

"Do you think there's a fire somewhere?"

"The alarms would be going off if there was. There was a big fire in town yesterday, so maybe it's residual from that."

"Maybe," I say, still feeling uncomfortable. The doors open, and a young firefighter in full gear stands waiting. I can't help but notice his tattered and scorched clothing.

Alex nods respectfully as he exits. "I hope nobody was hurt."

The firefighter enters the elevator and turns to face us. "Lives were lost, but we did the best we could."

The door closes, and Alex walks away. "Well, that explains why the elevator smells like a campfire."

I can't take my eyes off the elevator as the floors continue to show it going up. "How many floors does this hospital have?" I ask, intrigued.

"Not many." Alex turns to look for directory arrows to the room. "The room is this way. Maya? Are you coming?"

There was something ominous about that firefighter. The hair stands on the back of my neck as my sixth sense awakens, making me tingle with sensory overload. I hear my name through the momentary fog, which snaps me back to reality.

"Maya? Are you okay?"

"Yes," I say, embarrassed. "You did see that guy, right?"

"I did. I was talking to him. Are you sure you're okay?"

A nurse walks by, and I stop her. "Excuse me, how many floors does this hospital have?"

"Three, not including the basement."

I force a polite smile, trying to hide my unease. "Thank you."

She continues on her way, and Alex waits for me to catch up.

"What's going on?" he asks, concerned. "What's with the obsession with the number of floors?"

I hesitate, concerned if I tell him he'll think I'm crazy. "Did you notice when that firefighter got in the elevator, he went up...not down?"

"Maybe he was visiting patients on another floor?"

"Maybe." We find room three hundred and seven and walk in.

"But?"

"Alex, I know this is going to sound nuts, but it said it went up to the sixth floor."

"That's impossible."

He's right. It's impossible. But I saw what I saw. There's a loud bang as an orderly misjudges the width of the door as he pushes my mom's gurney into the room. I'm glad it interrupted what might have turned into a conversation that made me look unstable. We stand out of the way as they transfer her to the permanent bed.

A doctor whips into the room, flipping through papers on a clipboard. He looks up and acknowledges Alex and me before standing at the bedside. Her eyes flutter open, and he smiles. "Hi. I hear you're not feeling well."

"I've felt better," she says, struggling to keep her eyes open.

"I'm Doctor Fulton. You can call me Grant."

I raise my brow. "You're not Doctor Murray?"

"Oh, no. I'm much better looking," he jests.

He lightly touches my mom's hand, and she opens her eyes again. "Not all your test results are back yet, so Doctor Murray has left for the day."

"Are you kidding me?" I say, annoyed.

He glances over at me and then continues to talk to my mom. "He'll be in first thing in the morning. Until then, I will do my best to look after you and make you comfortable."

"I have questions," I say in a demanding tone. Alex reaches up and holds my elbow with a firm grip.

"Sorry, this is always a difficult time. It's best you speak to Doctor Murray in the morning. If your mom permits him to share her medical information with you, he can fill you in."

"If she permits him? I don't have the right to know what's going on?"

He frowns as his pager goes off. "I'm sorry, I'm afraid that's how it works with patient confidentiality. It sucks, I know. For now, I've given her something for the pain, which will make her sleepy. I suggest you go home and rest, then return in the morning."

"Yes, go home," Mom says, her eyes still closed.

I watch as Doctor Fulton leaves the room on a mission.

"Maya," she says groggily. "Go home. Be with Jack. I'll be fine."

Alex shrugs. "There won't be much you can do, and she's in good hands here."

I walk to the side of her bed and watch her sleep for a moment. "It doesn't feel right leaving her."

"For heaven's sake, Maya. Go home," she says, exasperated. "They have you as my emergency contact in case they need to call you, but I'm not going anywhere yet. I still have work to do in this world before I leave."

"Mom! Stop talking like that. You're freaking me out."

"It's true. Do you honestly think you're the only one with the gift? Where do you think you got it from?"

My eyes widen, and my chin drops. I cover my open mouth with my hands.

"What gift? What is she talking about?" Alex asks, confused.

Stunned, I drop my hands heavily to my side. "Nothing," I deny. "She's heavily medicated. She's just rambling nonsense now."

Alex narrows his eyes.

"I better get home. Jack will be home from school soon."

"What are you going to tell him?"

"Just that she's here and not feeling well. I don't know anything else until I talk to the oncologist."

Alex nods. "I'll take you home."

Jack is waiting outside when we pull into the driveway. He approaches the vehicle as I get out of the car. "What's wrong?" he asks, panicked. "Don't tell me it's nothing. I've had those anxious feelings all afternoon." He pauses, and his eyes open wide. "It's Grams, isn't it? Is she okay? What happened?"

I place my hands on the sides of his arms, trying to calm the brewing hysteria. "Jack, calm down. Grandma is okay, but she's in the hospital."

"I KNEW IT!" he screams as he tugs away from me. "You called him, but you didn't call me?"

Alex makes his way around the front of the vehicle. "Mom didn't call me, buddy. I was showing a house in the neighbourhood and saw the ambulance, so I stopped."

"They wouldn't let me go with her, so Alex drove me to the hospital. It was almost the end of your school day, so I figured I'd tell you when you got home. I didn't know you sensed something was wrong. I'm sorry."

"What happened to her?"

"She might have had a fall," Alex answers.

Jack looks to me for confirmation. "We don't know much yet because they're waiting on test results, so they're keeping her overnight."

He takes a deep breath and quickly glances at Alex.

Alex nods toward the door. "Come on, let's go in the house. Your mom has something to tell you."

My heart is pounding like a hammer in my chest. When Jack turns to follow Alex to the door, I close my eyes and exhale. I've had to deal with things alone for so many years. I'm grateful to have reinforcements tonight.

Chapter Seven

I have the office move all my morning appointments so I can go straight to the hospital. Mom is sleeping when I get there, and it doesn't look like she's had a great night. She's slumped over in a partially elevated bed with the blankets twisted and tangled around her legs.

Her silver-stranded hair hangs limply, covering her face. "Hi, Mom," I say softly, brushing it to the side.

Her head bobs as her neck strains to lift it. "Oh, good morning, dear," she says, seemingly pleased to see me.

"How are you feeling today?"

"Like a broken old woman with a few more battle wounds." She pulls up the side of her hospital gown to show me the bruises.

"Ouch. I'm assuming that's from when you hit the floor?"

"I suppose so. I don't remember what happened. I'm sorry, Maya. I didn't mean to bother you."

"You didn't bother me, Mom. I felt scared. I don't know how long you've been lying there. I stopped in because I hadn't heard from you in a few days, and you weren't answering the phone. Tell me you weren't laying there for two days."

"I honestly don't know."

Feeling my emotions starting to escalate, I pause. The last thing she needs right now is me losing it. "Well, that's not good. We'll have to figure something out when you go home so it doesn't happen again."

Mom looks past me at something, and I turn to see an older man wearing street clothes writing on the charts. Noting the pause in our conversation, he looks up.

"Good morning, Doctor," my mom says with a gravelly voice.

I help her take a sip of water while trying to keep my attention on him. He slipped into the room without me even noticing. I want to make sure he doesn't exit the same way until I have some answers.

"Good morning, Gladys. I see you've given your family a fright."

"That's an understatement," I add.

He walks to the side of the bed and checks the equipment around her.

"Are you in any pain?"

"I'm just stiff and sore from the fall."

He moves the blankets to peruse the damage. He cringes as he covers her back up. "That must have been a doozie of a fall."

I anxiously wait for the opportunity to jump into the conversation.

"I can see your daughter has many questions. I hope you've told her I strongly advised you to share your medical condition with your friends and family."

I shift my weight back and forth, feeling anxious. "She didn't."

He looks up and establishes eye contact with me. "Patients, during these times, need support. Not just with the day-to-day things but emotionally and psychologically."

"She's as stubborn as a mule."

He holds up his hand, stopping my soon-to-come barrage of questions. "Gladys, do I have your permission to discuss your medical condition and the treatment plans you've got in place with your daughter?"

My mom looks frustrated. "I didn't want to bother her with all this nonsense."

"MOM!"

She looks at me, startled by the tone in my voice.

Doctor Murray gently strokes her hand and smiles at her. "My friend, you've reached the time we discussed where you need your daughter's help. Let her be there for you."

She reluctantly nods, and he pats her hand. "I think you made the right decision." He gets to his feet and moves toward me, touching my arm. "Let's not have this conversation in the room."

I brace myself for what he's about to say as I follow him into the hall.

"This is not going to be easy to hear."

"I figured. Just tell me."

"Your mom has pancreatic cancer."

A wave of fear rolls through my body. "How long has she known?"

"She was referred to me four months ago by her family physician."

I purse my lips. "What can be done?"

"By the time she got to me, it was too far advanced for surgical options. We discussed treatments like chemo and radiation, but after getting all the facts and information, she decided that's not what she wants."

Rage pulses through my veins. "Well, I'll make her change her mind."

"I understand how you're feeling right now. I believe your mom is of sound mind and capable of deciding the course of her treatment. Chemotherapy and radiation are hard enough on young bodies, and all we may accomplish is that we extend the inevitable. She doesn't want to spend the little time she has left feeling sicker than she does already, only to add a few months to her life."

Tears well up in my eyes, and I can't fight it anymore. "So, she's dying."

"Yes." He passes me a box of tissue from a nearby supply cart.

"How long?"

"As far as I can see, she's severely dehydrated and probably hasn't eaten in days. I hope that once we correct that, she'll feel better and can go home. But her body is getting weaker, and given the advanced stage of the cancer, my best guess would be that she has a month to live. Maybe less."

I hold my hands over my face as I break down. "I can't believe this is happening," I say through my sobs.

Doctor Murray places his hand on my back to console me. "Is there someone you can call?"

I wipe my eyes and pull myself together. "I'll be fine. I'll call my sisters on my way to work."

"Be kind to yourself. If you can take the day off, I would do so. You need some time to process."

I nod.

"And remember, it was difficult for her to make the decisions she did. Don't be too hard on her."

I exhale harshly. "Okay. I've got this."

"You're as stubborn and strong as she is."

He's not wrong.

"I would try to talk her into moving in with you. Or the other way around. I don't think anyone should be alone during these times if they don't have to."

"I'll work on it. We've been trying to get her to move in for years."

"That doesn't surprise me. I'm sure I'll see you more over the next little while. If you think she may be experiencing pain, then speak up. She won't ask for painkillers, and there's no reason to endure it when we can make her more comfortable."

"Thank you." I watch as he walks to the nurse's station and picks up another clipboard. Pulling myself together and stepping back into the room takes every ounce of strength I have.

"Did he answer all your questions?" she asks when I return.

"Yes."

"Good. Could you help me find something good on this television? I need to drown out that old woman's jabbering. Honestly, the way she goes on, she probably died from lack of oxygen because she doesn't shut up."

I look around the room and confirm we're alone. It doesn't shock me that she's receiving visitors from beyond this life. I've never seen ghosts before, but when I walk down the hallway here, I'm not sure all the people around me are alive. "Let me see if I can figure it out." I pull the tablet around and use the touch screen to find the channel buttons. I search for some of her favourite shows and settle on a station. "Did you eat breakfast this morning?"

"A little. I don't have much appetite."

I frown at her.

"You're not going to start hassling me now, are you?"

"If it means that you get stronger so you can get out of this place and go home, then you can count on it."

"I'll try to eat more lunch."

"Good. I'll stay and make sure you do."

She watches ten minutes of television before she falls asleep. She's lost so much weight that she looks like a frail child almost lost in the bed. My phone vibrates, and I take it out of my pocket.

I feel comfort in seeing Alex's name on an incoming text message.

Alex: How's your mom?
Maya: Resting now.
Alex: Did you see the doctor?
Maya: Yes. It's not good. I'll call you later.
Alex: I can come to the hospital.

Maya: No, I'm ok. It's still sinking in. I may need a hug when I get home.
Alex: I'll be there. Call me when you leave.

The nurse administers what I suspect is a shot for the pain.

"She's going to be out for some time. If you plan to stay the morning, it's a good time to get a coffee or go for a walk and stretch your legs."

"Thank you. I need some fresh air, so I'll go out to my car and make phone calls. I'll be back in a bit."

I dial all three of my siblings on the way through the parking lot, but not one of them answers. I decide not to leave the details in a message, although I feel that's about all the sensitivity they deserve. I jump into the driver's seat, lean back, and close my eyes. Immediately, I start thinking about all the things I need to do to get my house ready for her when she comes home. My phone rings, making me jump. I answer it without even looking at the display.

"Hi, Maya. It's been a long time. I wasn't sure you'd take my call."

A nervous feeling rushes through my body, making my skin feel prickly. "Kevin?"

"Yes. How are you doing?"

I suddenly don't know any words. I struggle. "I...good." I place my palm on my forehead. "I'm good."

"And Jack?"

"He's fine. You'd know that if you ever called him."

"I know, I know. I'm a father failure."

"Why are you calling, Kevin?"

"I'm coming into town next week, and I need to talk to you and Jack about something important."

"Just tell me now so I can say no and save you the trouble."

"Maya, please. Don't be like that. This is important. I'll call you once I'm in town."

I hang up without saying anything else. Why does everything happen all at once? I walk back toward the hospital entrance. There's no point in waiting for my sisters to call me back; I feel like I've been out for a long time.

My mom's eyes flutter open when I enter the room. I smile, trying to give her some comfort. "Did you have a good rest?"

"I had the strangest dreams."

"Oh no. What about?"

"My room was full of children. But they were all wearing gruesome masks and costumes. I kept asking them to go, but they wouldn't leave."

I raise a brow. "That's creepy."

"It was horrible."

I lean over and kiss her on the forehead. "I'm sure it was what they gave you for the pain."

"I didn't like it." She looks past me.

"I'm sorry." I turn to see who entered the room.

"Jack!" she says, perking up.

"Hi, Grams."

I narrow my brow, and he answers my unasked question.

"Relax, Mother. I went to all my classes. I had a free period last, and I've already done my homework."

My mom mumbles something, and Jack looks at me, confused.

"It's part English, part Irish. She does it to me all the time these days."

"What did she say?"

"Something about...don't sass your mother. Sounds like good advice to me."

Her fingers tremble slightly as she reaches out, prompting Jack to move to her side. She grasps his hand and holds it tightly. "It's so nice that you've come." Her eyes close, and her body becomes languid as if the statement has exhausted her.

A nurse comes in to check her vitals and gives us a sympathetic smile. A cold chill fills the room. I can tell from Jack's expression that he feels it, too. He glances in my direction with an understanding that needs no explanation.

She walks around Jack to straighten the pillow and cover her with a blanket. "She needs rest for her body to fight it. Why don't you go home and take a break yourself? I'll take good care of her."

She disappears as she leaves the room, but I still feel her energy. "Let's let Grandma sleep."

Jack reluctantly releases her hand and whispers his goodbye, promising to return tomorrow. She doesn't respond.

"That nurse wasn't real. Was she?" Jack asks as we walk down the hall.

"No. You were pretty calm. Have you ever seen a ghost like that before?"

"No. Have you?"

"No, and I hope this is not a new gift. Grandma is seeing them, too. It must be this place."

"Grams is really bad, isn't she?" he asks as we wait for the elevator.

I place my hand on his back and nod. "I'm afraid so."

The elevator door opens, and we step inside. Jack pushes the button for the main floor and then leans against the wall.

I get a strange sensation in my stomach as the elevator moves, and all the buttons go dark. I start to panic. "Are we going up?"

Jack stands erect. "It feels like it." He pushes buttons on the panel, but nothing seems to work.

"Press the call button," I suggest, feeling more alarmed.

He glances at me as he presses it several times with no response. Finally, we abruptly stop, causing us to lose our balance. The door opens to what seems to be a vacant floor. Ice-cold fear floods my veins as I stare at the floor marker on the wall in front of me.

"That's strange," Jack says, noting there aren't six floors on the panel. "It smells like there was a fire or something. Maybe that's why they don't use this floor."

I respond when I'm finally able to breathe. "Maybe." The light in the elevator suddenly comes back on, and the panel flashes. "I wonder how this all works," he says, intrigued.

"Try the main floor again."

"Are you okay?" he asks, picking up on my unease as he pushes the button and the door closes. The main floor button lights up, and it feels like we're now travelling in the downward direction.

The doors open, and I shoot out like a bat out of hell. People in the lobby stop abruptly and stare at me, startled by my exit.

"Great." Jack shows his annoyance. "Now they probably think I farted in the elevator."

I take long, deep breaths of fresh air as we walk to the SUV, trying to calm my nerves. Jack climbs in beside me as if nothing has phased him.

"Did you not feel anything back there on the elevator?" I ask curiously.

"Like what?"

"I don't know. Dread. Unrest."

"Death," he replies unfazed.

I swallow hard.

"I felt it. I also just saw a ghost taking care of my grandmother. I'm still processing, but I guess it doesn't scare me like it does you."

"You're lucky." I pull out of the parking lot.

"How long does she have?" He finally asks.

"The doctor doesn't know for sure. It depends on how long her body can fight it. She's refused treatments, so it could be months."

"Something tells me it's more like weeks."

I reach over and hold his hand. "Hey, have you heard from your dad lately?"

"Not in a while."

"He's coming for a visit."

"Why?"

I shrug. "He said he has something important to talk to us about."

"Alex is here!" Jack says excitedly when he sees him waiting on the porch with a box from our favourite local bakery. I feel a great sense of relief to see him myself.

"I hope those are butter tarts!" I walk toward him.

"You know me so well."

"Sweet!" Jack takes the box out of Alex's hand. "I'll take them into the house."

"Don't eat them all!" I holler.

Alex extends his arms, and I walk straight into them, unleashing a flood of emotion. He wraps himself around me and lowers his cheek to mine. "I'm so sorry."

We stand there for a long time saying nothing but understanding everything. "We better get inside and save ourselves a tart." He studies my tear-stained face as he pulls away and wipes the damp trails. "I've got you," he assures me with an empathetic smile. "You and Jack."

Chapter Eight

It's a long walk down the hospital corridor to my
mother's room. I'm a little unnerved when I find the room
empty and the bed made as if she was never there. Nurses
and personal care support workers lift their eyes as I walk
past, but no one offers any information. My heart begins to
race as I approach the nurse's station. Half a dozen people
buzz around the desk area, all looking like they're working on
something important. No one acknowledges me. I clear my
throat, but not one person looks in my direction. A woman
dressed in street clothes emerges from an office behind the
counter. She pauses and raises her brow, waiting for me to
speak.

"I'm looking for my mom. She was in room three
hundred and seven."

"Her name?"

"Gladys Dunn."

She takes several steps toward the desk and flips
through some papers before turning to her computer
monitor. "We moved her to F wing. Follow the blue footprints
on the floor down the hall to the end and turn left. There will
be signs. Check with the nursing station there."

I nod and look down at the floor as I follow the blue
footprints painted there. It seems like the longest walk ever.

Like someone keeps moving the double doors at the end of the hall, ensuring I never reach them. The signs on the wall finally become legible.

F wing – Palliative care. I feel lightheaded and concentrate on breathing so I don't pass out.

A young nurse at the desk looks up as I come through the door. Concerned, she rounds the desk and walks toward me.

"Are you okay?"

I'm not sure if I am or not. I shake my head. "Yes. It was a long walk."

"This hospital has more wings than an octopus has tentacles." She smiles and walks back toward the nurse's station. "How can I help you?"

"I'm looking for Gladys Dunn. They said she was moved here."

"Are you her daughter?"

"Yes, I'm Maya."

"She's doing much better today." She walks down a short hallway, and I follow. "She's even up and had some breakfast."

I enter the room behind her and find my mom sitting in a wheelchair, watching television.

"Gladys, your daughter is here." She stops and waits for me to catch up. "She wasn't too impressed we made her get up and get dressed," she says with a smile. "She gave us a pretty hard time."

"That doesn't surprise me. I'm so sorry. She looks much better than the last time I saw her."

"Let me know if there's anything you need."

I place my jacket and purse on the chair as she leaves. "I will, thank you."

I feel some of the pressure lift from my chest. I lean over her and kiss her on the head. "Hi, Mom. You look like you're doing better today."

"I'm still a bit stiff. The nurse said it might take a few days."

"She seems nice."

"A lot nicer than those other miserable sods."

"Mom!"

"It's true. They need a refresher course on kindness and patience. If they don't have it in them, they've chosen the wrong career."

She's not wrong. And, as always...very blunt. We spent the morning chatting as if we were sitting at home in the garden. The feeling of impending doom begins to loosen its hold on me.

My phone rings, and I realize it's almost noon. Mom's eyes are heavy, and she struggles to stay awake.

"Who is it?"

"It's Alex. I can call him back."

"Nonsense. Take your call."

Reluctantly, I answer his call. "Hey."

"How are you?"

"I'm good. I'm at the hospital."

"I was calling to see if you wanted me to take you over."

"I couldn't sleep, so I came over early."

"How's she doing?"

"Remarkably well today. She was dressed and sitting in a chair when I got here."

"That's a great sign."

"And she's very chatty."

"I'm glad. She's getting stronger."

"It seems so. No sign of a doctor yet."

"So, no idea yet when she can come home?"

I pause, trying to stall the emotion welling up inside me. "They moved her to the palliative care wing."

"Oh. Well, they're better equipped to help her right now. The medical wing is understaffed and way too busy. I'm sure that's the only reason."

I wish I believed him, but I know better.

"Listen, Maya. Just forget about the awards banquet tonight. You've got too much going on."

My chin drops. "Is that tonight?" I search through the events on my phone. "I've lost track of the days."

"It is. But don't give it another thought. I understand. You should be with your family right now."

I glance over at my mom and she's closed her eyes. "I don't want to miss it."

"It's fine. Listen, I have an incoming call I need to take. You take care of your mom. I'll call you later."

"Okay. Bye." I hang up, feeling disappointed.

"Don't you dare think you're hanging around here tonight instead of going out with that strapping young man!" She opens her eyes and stares at me. "Do you hear me, girl?"

I try not to laugh. "Yes, ma'am."

"You go to that party and have yourself a good time. I don't want you hanging around tonight bugging me when all my shows are on the television. I'll still be here in the morning. Pass me my purse."

I hand her the small black bag and watch as she unfolds her wallet and takes out a wad of cash.

"Here," she says, peeling off a few hundred dollars. "Go buy yourself a new dress."

"I don't need your money," I protest. "And why are you carrying around that much cash on you?"

Her Irish brogue thickens. "I tucked it in my wallet a few days ago. A little birdie told me you were going to need it. Don't give me a hard time, Maya. I can't take it with me, and you can't go out with Alex in a dress you've had in the closet since the nineties."

"It's not that old, and how did you know I still have my graduation dress?" I take the money reluctantly. "I don't even know where to shop for dresses in town."

"You better figure it out quickly. I didn't win your father over wearing a dress from Walmart, dear."

I scratch my head.

"Go!"

"But the doctor hasn't been in yet."

"He won't be in today, Maya. It's Saturday. Besides, he won't have anything to say that we don't already know. Get out!"

"Geez, okay." I lean down and hug her in the wheelchair, then pick up my things and head toward the door. "Love you, Mom."

"Maya,"

I stop and turn toward her.

"Don't feck it up this time."

I roll my eyes. "I'll call you later."

The elevator still has a faint smoky aroma to it. As I step in, the hair stands on the back of my neck. I watch the numbers carefully, making sure they descend in the proper order as it makes its way to the ground floor. I don't know what I'm reacting to or what I expect might happen, but I leave feeling relieved that there were no unexpected stops.

I head to historic downtown Orangeville to a small boutique I've noticed on my way to work. The display in the window is very trendy, and I hesitate before going in.

"Looking for something in particular?" the salesclerk asks from the back of the room.

"A dress, I think. I have an awards dinner to attend tonight."

"Take a look at the rack on the wall to your left. I'll be over in a minute."

I skim through the rack, sliding dresses to the left as I go. "Too fancy. Too small. Too widow-y." I pull out one that looks promising and hold it against myself. "Ugh. Too desperate." I frown as I look in the mirror.

"No luck?" the saleswoman asks when she finally approaches.

"I can't seem to find the right one."

She walks to a rack a few feet down. "I heard you talking to yourself." She pulls out a black and white dress and walks toward me. "Try this one."

I hold it up and smile until I flip over the price tag. "Holy Cow!"

"Just try it," she urges.

I enter the change room reluctantly. Even if I love it, I can't see myself spending that much money on a dress. I slip it over my head and let it fall past my hips. The material is silky soft and flows like a gown made for a grand ball. It feels amazing. I look at myself in the mirror, trying to find a flaw or a reason to put it back on the rack. I fail.

I hand the money from my mom to the cashier and pay the balance on my credit card. I swallow hard when it rings up as a *final sale.* "Geezus. That's the sale price?"

The cashier hands me a fancy paper bag full of tissue paper. "It is. I guess today is your lucky day."

I shake my head as I leave the store, still in shock. I dial Alex's number as I walk to the car.

"Hey!"

"Hi. What time are you picking me up tonight?"

"I didn't think you would be up to coming."

I note a strange tone in his voice and stop walking. "Oh. Did you already ask someone else?"

"NO! I didn't want to go with anyone but you. Are you sure you're up to it?"

I unlock my car door and toss the bag onto the passenger seat. "Well, I just bought a dress that cost more than I spent on groceries for the month. So, I'm sure."

I can hear the excitement in his voice. "That's great. Cocktails start at six, so I'll pick you up about thirty minutes before that."

"I'll see you then."

"I can't wait to see this dress."

Jack is rummaging through the kitchen cupboards when I get home. "When are you going grocery shopping?" he asks, searching for something to eat.

I look down at my fancy bag and feel guilty. "Call and order a pizza." I hand him my bank card. "I forgot tonight is Alex's award dinner."

"Are you going?" he asks curiously.

"Yes. He's picking me up. Will you be okay home by yourself tonight?"

"Is that a trick question? I'm almost seventeen."

I purse my lips and sigh. "Of course, sorry. I don't know where my head is."

"What's in the bag."

My cheeks begin to feel warm, and Jack raises his brow. "I bought a new dress."

"No way! You? Spent money on a dress?"

"Stop it. I spend money on myself."

"When?"

"Sometimes."

"Pfft. No times."

I stand with my hands on my hips and answer defensively. "Well...this time."

"You like Alex," he teases.

I wrinkle my nose. "Yeah. I kind of like him."

"Me too."

Chapter Nine

A sudden wave of nervousness washes over me as I clasp my earring and stand to look at myself in the mirror.

I jump when Jack hollers up the stairs. "Alex is here!"

I carefully manoeuvre the stairs in my heels, and Alex stares at me open-mouthed when I reach the bottom. "You're absolutely stunning."

"I feel stunning."

He takes my jacket out of my hand and holds it out for me. "It's a shame to cover up such a beautiful dress," he says as he sweeps my hair from under the collar. "But there's a chill in the air tonight."

"This sounds like a segue to a Phil Collins song."

"I thought about it." Alex opens the door, and my bout of nerves turns to excitement. "Ready?" He takes my hand and helps me down the front step.

"Yes."

"Good, because I can't wait to show you off tonight."

The front door swings open behind me, startling me. "Were you even going to say goodbye?" Jack asks, amused.

"I'm sorry," I say, feeling the guilt of my parenting failure. "Are you sure you're going to be okay?"

Jack looks at Alex with a raised brow. "Can you believe her?"

Alex shrugs and tries to hide his amusement.

"Okay, I get it. Text me if you need anything."

"I'll be fine. Don't hurry home."

Before I can answer, he closes the door and locks it. "Man, he's stubborn."

Alex purses his lips. "Mmhmm."

I narrow my eyes, and he immediately holds up his hands. "I didn't say a word."

"But you thought it. I can tell."

He smirks as he opens the car door. "Did I mention how stunning you look tonight?"

Lucky for him, I still find him charming.

"You better stick close to me tonight. That perfume will have all the men following you around."

I'm pleased with his reaction. He closes the door, and as I wait for him to get in beside me, I lift the collar of my jacket to my nose and inhale the subtle flowery perfume I dabbed on sparingly. It's alluring and persuasive. He should be worried.

"Are you up for any awards tonight?" I ask on the ride there.

"I am. Salesman of the year."

"Oh, that's exciting."

"It's nerve-racking. It's based on several things. Number of homes sold. Number of homes sold over asking. Overall sales and commissions."

"That's better than based on popularity."

"Agreed, but the nice guy often finishes last in sales. I've had a tough year with a colleague who has withheld leads and stolen business."

"He sounds like a dick."

"He is. I come across a lot of them in this business. Those who stretch the truth and use every loophole possible to further their financial gain. It's often not in the best interest of their client."

I catch him glancing at me several times before he pulls up to the hall entrance where the dinner is being held. "Wow!" I say, impressed. "I didn't even know there was someplace this fancy in town."

Alex opens the car door and extends his hand. "Wait for me inside, out of the cold air. I'll park and meet you inside."

I step inside the grand lobby and suddenly feel small and insignificant. People wander around in every direction, exchanging what seems to be insincere greetings and well wishes. A handsome man approaches, and I feel he is familiar to me, but I can't place him.

He extends his hand. "Hello. I'm David. Are you looking for someone?"

"Hi, I'm Maya. I'm here with Alex. He's just parking the car."

The door opens, and Alex steps into the building. His smile fades when he sees us. His eyes are laser-focused on David as he approaches. I'm intrigued by his reaction.

"Hello, Alex," David says, extending his hand.

"I see you've met Maya." He looks down at David's outreached hand and doesn't respond.

David drops his hand to his side. "I have, yes. But then, who wouldn't be drawn to the most beautiful woman in the room."

Alex helps me remove my coat and hands it to the girl in the coat check a few feet away.

"I recognize you," I say to David. "I think our kids played soccer together when they were younger."

Returning to my side, Alex reaches for my hand before he can respond. "Let's find our seats, shall we." He shoulders past David, and his eyes locked to his in an unmistakable silent warning. Halfway across the room, he places his hand on the small of my back. "I see I can't leave you alone for five minutes."

"Are you going to tell me what that was all about?"

He ushers me through the candlelit room to a table and holds out my chair. "No."

"He seemed nice enough."

"Trust me; he's not a good guy."

"Oh, is he the dick?" I pause and study his body language. "Wait. Are you jealous?"

"No."

I smile. "You are. You're jealous."

There's a moment as I look into his eyes when I'm certain I can see straight through to his soul. My heart starts to beat with a strange ardour. He looks as if there's something he wants to say, and the anticipation has me on edge.

"Just stay away from him."

My hopes for a romantic confession crash as he picks up a bottle of wine and pours us each a glass. The room around us fills up quickly. Alex still seems to be on edge. He hardly contributes to the conversation at the table during dinner.

I place my hand on his knee, hoping the gesture will help him centre his energy and focus on something else. His shoulders soften, and then he places his hand on top of mine as he turns to me. "I'm sorry about earlier."

I smile. "It's fine."

"That guy just gets to me. There's this ridiculous rivalry between us, and when I saw him with you…"

I raise my brow and smile. "You were jealous."

He fidgets uncomfortably. "I was jealous."

I lean in and place my cheek upon his, then whisper. "You don't need to be." I don't know what comes over me. I'm usually not into public displays of affection, but I gently kiss his lips. As I move away, I search his eyes. "Can I ask you a question?"

"Sure, but it's never a good sign if you ask first."

"Did you walk up to me the last night of lacrosse because you needed answers, or was there more to it?"

Alex leans back in his chair, hesitant to answer.

"You must have seen us there before if you were at every game. In all these years, you never stopped by the house to bring my mom tea."

"For many years, I figured it was best to let sleeping dogs lie. Kevin was never with you, and I'd heard rumours, but I didn't know if you were still married. Since you never made any attempts to search me out, I figured our time had passed."

The venue staff clears the dishes from the table.

"So then, what changed?"

"I ran into your mom in town a few days before. It was strange, actually. I thought she was stalking me up and down the aisles of the grocery store."

I sigh. "She probably was."

"Well, she told me that you'd love to see me again and that I should come and say hello."

I nod my understanding. "Now it all makes sense. Remind me later to look up how to say *meddling pain in the ass* in Irish."

"I did stop by your house that night because I needed to know what happened. I needed to know because I still have feelings for you. And if you walked away because you didn't have feelings for me, I didn't want to get my hopes up. My heart couldn't take it."

"I guess I owe Mom a huge thank you."

He reaches for my hand. "I might not have ever approached you if it weren't for her encouragement. And as for taking her a tea, it was simply an excuse to drop by in hopes of running into you again."

I've had just enough wine, and I'm ready to tell him I still have feelings for him, too, when the lights come on just enough so presenters can safely see their way to the stage.

The ceremony begins, and I pour Alex another glass of wine, suspecting that David is his closest competitor for salesman of the year. I feel eyes upon me from the other side of the room, and when I glance in that direction, I find David smiling at me. He raises his glass as if he's wishing us success. An evil grin appears on his lips as he swallows the contents in one gulp. The gesture leaves me believing Alex is right. He's not a good guy. I tear my attention away and focus on the speaker while feeling his stare from across the room.

It feels like we've been waiting for hours, but we've finally reached the final award—Salesman of the Year. Alex tenses beside me, and I reach for his hand and grip it tightly. It takes every ounce of energy I have not to establish eye contact with his opponent on the other side of the room.

The waiting is torturous. "Just announce the winner already," I plead under my breath.

"ALEX THOMAS!"

The room erupts in celebratory cheers and applause. I stand as Alex gets to his feet and wraps his arms around me before making his way to the stage. I feel overwhelming pride and happiness as he graciously accepts his award and gives the thank you speech, which I'm sure he's been rehearsing for days.

I glance across the room and find David staring at me. I smile, raise my glass, and finish the contents in one gulp. I find my response quite satisfying.

Alex leaves the stage with his award, stops to shake hands, and accepts congratulations on returning to the table. My brow raises when a particular redhead at the front of the room embraces him and engages in a kiss completely inappropriate for coworkers. "What the fuck?" I murmur. Then it hits me like a ton of bricks. It can't be. I tap the arm of the woman sitting next to me. "Do you know who that woman is?"

"Hilary Jones."

Adrenaline jolts through my system like a flash of lightning, ruining the calming effects of the wine. My first reaction is to flee, but before I can act, Alex reaches the table. He pulls me into his arms and whispers into my ear. "Please let me explain."

"Oh, I can't wait to hear this."

"Not here. Let's get some air." He ushers me into the lobby and finds a quiet spot to be alone. "I'm sorry."

I laugh once. "So am I."

"I should have told you she was going to be here."

"Yup, a heads up would have been nice." I struggle with making eye contact with him right now.

"Maya?" He reaches for my arm, and his firm grip demands my acknowledgement. I look up.

"Would you have come if you knew?"

I think about it for a moment. The answer is absolutely NOT.

"I wanted to share this moment with you. It was important to me. I know I should have prepared you."

"Do you have any idea what it was like watching that? It was like walking into high school and finding you two together all over again."

He strokes my arms in a consoling manner. "I know. I know. I suck. I wasn't thinking." He pauses and smiles.

I'm confused by his reaction. "What?"

"You're jealous."

I roll my eyes. "No, I'm not."

"You just busted my balls about being jealous of David. Are you going to deny it?"

"I need more wine." I turn to walk away, but he grabs my arm and tightens his grip, stopping me.

I turn to look at him. "Really?" I say, feeling annoyed. The look in his eyes paralyzes me as he pulls me against his body. His hand gently brushes my hair away from my face and then traces his fingertip over my lips. As he advances, the warmth of his breath and the lingering fruity fragrance of the house wine sends all rational thoughts fleeting from my mind.

The first brush of his lips is a gentle pass of affection—sweet and tender. I've been waiting for this moment, and it leaves me wanting more. Alex responds, anchoring me firmly against his body and claiming me with unreserved want and desire. It's both what I've been craving and what I've been afraid of since the first moment I saw him.

I stare at his lips when he slowly moves away, hoping for their return. He gently raises my chin with his finger until our eyes meet. "You don't need to feel jealous. You're the only woman in that room I want to kiss." A confident smile forms on his lips, and I feel like my lungs can welcome air again. "Let's go back in for another drink and then get out of here."

I step away, and he loosens his grip, letting me go. I hold up one finger. "One more drink."

He escorts me into the room and leaves me at the empty table while he goes to the bar. My stomach is in knots, and I suddenly understand why. Hilary pulls out the chair beside me and sits. "Maya, right?"

I purse my lips and nod. She knows damn well who I am.

"I haven't seen you since high school. I just moved back to town. Wait…you're not a real estate agent, are you?"

"No. I'm a physiotherapist."

Confused, she squints her eyes.

"I'm here with Alex."

She raises her brow and blinks rapidly. "Oh, he didn't mention that. So, you two are…" She shakes her head. "I'm sorry, I thought that ship had sailed."

Undaunted, I lock eyes with her. "And yet, here we are back at the dock."

Her neck becomes red and blotchy. A reaction caused by nerves, no doubt. Poor thing. Alex watches nervously from across the room while he waits in line at the bar. I'm about to add to her stress. "Can I ask you a question?"

"Sure."

"Back in high school. Did you and Alex…" I pause.

"Have a thing?"

"Yes, was there something between you? Romantically, I mean."

She frowns. "You were all he talked about."

I'm throwing the bullshit flag. "I walked into the library one day and found you kissing."

She laughs. "No, you walked in and found me trying to elicit a kiss from him. But he wasn't interested."

I narrow my eyes. "Not even after I was out of the picture?"

"Girl, you left him so broken-hearted nobody had a chance. Why do you think he's still single?"

I'm stunned. I blink rapidly, trying to get my head around it.

A firm hand squeezes my shoulder. "Sorry to interrupt," David says. "Jack is your son, right?"

"Yes!"

"I remember you now. Hilary, can I borrow you for a moment?"

"Of course." She picks up her purse and forces a smile. "Don't break his heart again."

A tightness in my chest makes my heart hurt as they walk away.

"Is everything okay?" Alex asks when he returns.

"Fine. Where are the drinks?"

"I gave up waiting in line when I saw David heading in this direction."

"Well, you don't have to worry about him anymore."

"Why's that?"

I nod toward the corner where David and Hilary are engaged in an intimately close conversation.

"Oh!" Alex says, surprised.

"Apparently, David decided it would get under your skin more if he showed interest in Hilary instead of me."

Alex shrugs. "He was wrong. Would you mind if we got out of here?"

"I'm okay with not seeing Hilary or David anymore tonight."

"I don't have to take you home. We could go back to my place for a drink."

"Sure, that's fine with me. I'm done peopling for today."

He places his hand on my back and steers me toward the coat check. "I'm done too. I'm looking forward to spending some time alone with you."

As he helps me with my coat, he brushes his cheek against my neck, and I suspect he's taking advantage of the moment to appreciate my perfume.

I hope the stars are finally aligned for Alex and me tonight. I don't think it's a coincidence that he suddenly popped back into my life after all these years. There are strong forces at work here.

Chapter Ten

The stars shine brightly in the clear evening sky, illuminating the parking lot. "They're almost as beautiful as you tonight," Alex says, opening my car door. "It's a shame you won't get your money's worth out of that dress."

I grunt. "If I want to get my money's worth out of this dress, I'll have to be buried in it so I can continue wearing it in the afterlife."

He's still chuckling when he climbs into the driver's seat beside me. "I missed your sense of humour."

"My only charm."

"Not true. You have many."

I blush and look away, feeling embarrassed by my reaction. It makes the short drive feel like hours.

"Here we are."

"Not at all what I was expecting." I get out of the car and walk toward the older home. Alex looks at me curiously.

"What were you expecting?" He opens the door and welcomes me in.

My eyes dart around the room. "I don't know. Something trendy and bougie. Like a modern condominium with a gym and lots of amenities."

Alex flips on the lights and turns to me with a wounded look.

I look around the room. "It's just an updated version of the house you grew up in."

He nods. "Yeah. Because I have wonderful memories of that home. Great things happened there."

He gestures for my coat.

"I'm sorry. I hope I didn't…"

"Don't worry about it. I know what you mean. Realtors are often…bougie."

I follow him into the living space.

"What do you think now?"

"It's beautiful. Warm and inviting."

"I was going for comfort." He directs me to the huge sectional couch in the middle of the room.

Glad to finally be off my feet, I sit. "This is comfy."

He sits beside me, and a mischievous grin forms on his lips. I narrow my eyes. "What are you up to?"

"There's something I want to do." He reaches down, grabs my feet, and pulls them onto his lap, forcing me to flip sideways.

"What are you doing?" I ask as I awkwardly lay beside him. He runs his hands across my thigh and down my leg, stopping at my ankle.

"These look very uncomfortable." He gently pries my shoes off my feet. I wiggle my toes, celebrating the freedom.

"Better?"

"Much better," I admit.

"I thought so. Comfortable is the goal for the overall mood in this room."

"Pretty shoes are seldom comfortable," I admit.

He massages my feet with strong hands, and I hold back my moans of pleasure.

"Guess what?"

"What?" I ask, supporting myself on my elbows.

"It's my house, and I'm picking the movie."

He snatches the remote from the table before I can even sit up in this fancy dress. "That's not fair."

"It's still a win."

I pout, but he only finds it more humorous. I struggle to sit up, so he extends his hand to support me. Taking it, I swing my legs over the edge of the cushion and pull myself back into an upright position. He channel surfs, looking for something to watch. I take the remote out of his hand and place it back on the table. I'm not the least bit interested in watching television at the moment.

Alex studies me, and I begin to feel self-conscious. "Is there something else you'd like to do?"

I stare at his lips. I don't know if it's the wine or they're moving closer. I lean in to meet him, and when our lips finally meet, I feel like I've gone back in time to the carnival. My heart racing, butterflies in my stomach and the desire to explore further.

"I'll have more of that," I whisper as he slowly pulls away.

"I've learned a lot since we were teenagers," he says proudly.

"Really? Because I heard I ruined you for all other girls, so who have you been practicing with?"

Strong arms wrap around me, pulling me closer until his lips find mine again. This time, he claims me harder, deeper. His tongue dancing passionately with mine.

His strong hands explore my body over silk and lace until nothing, but the touch of skin on skin will sate his growing desire. A low feral growl prompts my lashes to flutter open.

He gets to his feet, his eyes widening like a predator locked on his prey. "Upstairs. First door on the right. I've been waiting seventeen years for this, and if I have to wait one more second, I will rip you out of that five-hundred-dollar dress."

I don't waste a moment, aware that he's a half step behind me as I climb the stairs. When I reach the bedside, I sweep my hair to the side and glance at him over my shoulder. As he accepts my invitation, the warmth of his breath on my neck heightens my arousal. Anticipation resonates in the air around us as he slowly unzips me. It's what we've both been longing for.

My dress falls to the floor, and he forces me to turn and face him. He takes a long, appreciative look at my body, paying particular attention to the curve of my breasts. I feel both vulnerable and empowered at the same time. I force my lips against him, deepening the kiss and stoking desire as I breathe in his air.

"Why are you still standing?" he growls, sweeping me off my feet and tossing me onto the bed. Hard, thick, and pulsing, he stands before me and unzips his pants, releasing himself from the uncomfortable constraint. When he climbs in on top of me, his heavily muscled body presses me into the mattress as he whispers in my ear. "I've been craving you all evening."

His lips brush across my jawline before claiming my mouth. His desperate kisses become more intense; demanding. He explores every inch of me, and I arch my body, seeking more of his warm, roaming tongue.

Alex's self-control starts to unravel, and I prepare myself for a rough possession as he settles between my thighs. The first thrust of his hips makes me gasp, and then silence falls between us as our gaze locks in a tender moment.

Supporting his weight on heavily muscled forearms, he buries his face in my neck. Every stroke has purpose.

Desire vibrates inside me, right down to my clit. I clench around him, trying to sate the ache there. I protest his withdrawal as he adjusts his position and, without notice, effortlessly flips our bodies over so that he's now lying beneath me.

Straddling him, I try to execute an exchange of power. Grasping my hips, he pulls me down, reminding me he's still in control. It doesn't matter. The feeling is so intense and so deep that friction holds me captive. I've never experienced anything like this before. Alex controls the rhythm and sets a punishing pace. With each downward stroke, he sinks deeper and deeper until there's no space between us. We are one.

Alex rolls to the side until I'm on my back again and pinned beneath him. He owns me with every thrust. A stimulating charge courses through us, and I cry out as wave after wave of pleasure pulses through my body. Alex curses as his hips jerk against me one last time before I receive his warm release.

After a few moments, he gently rolls to the side, releasing me from the heavy weight of his body. I lay against his chest, trying to calm my thundering pulse. "Well, those are new moves."

"Did you like that?" he asks, amused.

"I did. Couldn't you tell? I *really* liked it, actually."

He brushes my hair away from my face. "Oh, good. Wait until you see what I have planned for round two."

"Round two?"

"Mmhm."

"You can't possibly have anything left in the tank for another round."

"Oh, but I do, and I've been planning this for seventeen years."

I'm not sure if I should be afraid or excited. "Fuck me," I exclaim.

"That's the plan. As many times and as many ways as possible."

Chapter Eleven

There'd be a spring in my step if my muscles weren't so sore this morning. I admit Alex's stamina is impressive. I momentarily entertain the idea of joining a fitness program, but I know I'll never go. Besides, I much prefer the workout I had last night if I'm being completely honest.

I'm looking forward to seeing my mom this morning. She'll want to know all about my night out. I'll leave out the X-rated details, but somehow, I think she'll know just by looking at me.

I walk softly into the dark room so I don't startle her. She flutters open her eyes as I near the side of her bed and reaches for my hand. "Did you have a good time, Maya?"

"I did, Mom. I had a wonderful time."

She closes her eyes and then pauses before opening them again. I'm concerned that she's already spent her energy.

"Did you finally kiss the boy?" she says with a strained voice.

I laugh once and try to hide my blush. "Yes, Mom. I kissed him."

She lets go of my hand, dropping her arm heavily onto the bed.

"Good. It's about time."

My phone rings, and I roll my eyes as I answer. "Hi, Kevin." I glance at my mom, and she's closed her eyes again, so I quietly make my way to the door so I don't disturb her.

"I just called to ask if you could pick me up at the airport when I arrive."

I'm a little dumbfounded that he'd have the nerve to ask me for any kindness, but he is my son's father, so I should play nice. "As long as you give me enough notice so I can manage my work schedule."

"I'll send you my flight details. I arrive this afternoon."

I place my hand on my forehead and try to keep calm. "That's not enough notice, Kevin. I can't just reschedule patients without notice. Maybe you should take a cab."

He replies with a melancholy tone. "Please, Maya. Things have gotten a little more *desperate*. I have to make this trip sooner than originally planned. I'll explain everything when I get there. It's important."

I purse my lips, angry at myself for giving in, but it is Sunday, and we're closed, so there's no good reason why I can't. It just bugs me. "Okay, I'll do it."

"Thank you. I can't wait to see you again. Does Jack know I'm coming?"

"I'm pretty sure I mentioned it, but honestly, that should have come from you."

There's a long silence. "I haven't been the best dad. I regret that. I can only try harder going forward."

My mom calls my name, and I peek around the curtain. "I have to go. My mom is in the hospital, and she's calling for me. Don't forget to send me your flight details." I hang up without waiting for a reply.

"Maya?"

"I'm here, Mom. What's wrong?"

"Was there a fire?"

"A fire? In the hospital? I don't believe so."

"A young man came to visit me last night. He was wearing a firefighter's uniform."

"Oh." I furrow my brow. "Maybe there's a new program where random firefighters go room to room to visit with the patients?"

She scowls at me. "No, Maya. He left me something." She rummages through the stuff on her bedside table and becomes frustrated. "Now, where did that go? It was right here."

"What was it? I'll help look."

I sort and organize the stuff that has accumulated there.

"It was a thing."

"A thing?"

"A paper."

"Like a letter?"

"No, like a brochure."

"For what?"

"I don't know," she says flustered. "I need to find it. It was important."

I'm alarmed at how agitated she's getting, so I try to de-escalate things. "It's okay. It couldn't have gone far, so I'm sure it will show up."

She stares at me like she's looking straight through me. Like I'm not even there. It unnerves me enough that I turn to see if there's someone in the room behind me. "Mom?"

She blinks a few times and snaps out of it. "Bloody people always wandering into my room."

"I was saying don't worry about the paper. It'll show up."

She smiles and nods. I should feel relieved, but to be honest, I'm a little spooked.

"Who was on the phone, dear?"

"It was Kevin. Remember I said he was coming into town and wants to talk to Jack and me about something?"

"Yes."

"Well, he arrives later today, and I need to pick him up at the airport."

"Well, you shouldn't spend your time here then. I'm sure you have lots of things to do today. Like, go home and think about last night and how silly you were to let Alex get away the first time and how not to let it happen again."

I roll my eyes. "Mom, there is no chance that Kevin will sweep me off my feet and away from Alex again."

"I hope not." She closes her eyes. "Would you do something for me?"

I can't shake the feeling that we're being watched right now. I walk to the window and look around outside. "Of course!"

"If it's not too much to ask, could you stop by the house and check my gardens? I'm worried about my roses."

My shoulders soften. "Yes, I'll do that for you."

Her voice becomes sorrowful. "I'm going to miss that garden." I turn to find her with tears in her eyes.

I furrow a brow. "You'll be home soon enough."

"I don't think so, Maya."

"Stop." I insist. "When the oncologist comes in tomorrow, we'll ask what arrangements we need to make for you to go home. Maybe you'll have to come to stay with Jack and me until you regain your strength, but you won't have to stay here."

She starts to protest, but I stop her with a steely glare. I lean forward and kiss her on the forehead. "Rest. I'll go pick up Jack, and we'll go tend to the garden."

"I love you, Maya."

I smile and squeeze her hand. "I love you, too."

"Maya!" She reaches for my hand as I begin to walk away. "Don't be afraid to hit those feckin crows with the shovel."

I laugh all the way to the parking lot. When I get home, I sit in the car and check my messages while I wait for Jack. I'm not going to have much time to look after the garden. I quickly text my siblings about Mom's progress and ask once again that they visit soon. I look up as Jack gets in the car. "Your dad comes in at three P.M. We'll stop by Grandma's and check on the garden."

We drive silently most of the way, and I'm not sure why it feels so awkward. He gets out of the car and walks toward the backyard. I almost run into the back of him as he stops abruptly a few feet in. "What's wrong?"

He stands to the side to let me pass. My stomach twists, and I get a strange feeling prickling across my skin. "What's going on here?" I pull a wilted rose from a branch and inspect it closer.

"Do you smell smoke?" Jack asks. "They look almost singed."

"That's strange. Maybe someone had a backyard fire that got out of control." I look around the yard for other signs of smoke damage or soot but find nothing.

Jack walks to the back of the house. "I'll get the hose out. We better give everything a good watering."

"Agreed." I wander around the yard, and I'm perplexed that this strange phenomenon has only affected the roses. Everything else looks lush and healthy. "Maybe it's some kind of aphid that only roses get?"

Jack shrugs. "I suppose I can do some research later."

"That would be great unless you're busy with your dad."

He looks up and scowls. "I doubt that's the reason he's coming. I spend more quality time with Alex than him."

I nod. "You like Alex, don't you?"

"I do. He's a great guy, and we have a lot in common. I like having him around."

"So, you'd be okay if he was around more often?" I smile. "I kind of like him too."

Jack turns off the water and begins to wind up the hose. "I'm not a kid. I know what's going on between you two. I'm okay with it."

I grin. "I'm still getting used to you being all grown up."

He shakes his head in disapproval. "Could you make things any more awkward?"

"Sorry." I fail at holding back my amusement. Frustrated, he walks out of the yard and gets in the car.

Alex texts as I follow, causing me to pause and respond.

Maya: I'll call you later. We're on our way to pick up Jack's dad from the airport.
Alex: I'm sorry, I didn't know that was today.
Maya: It was a surprise to all of us.

Jack leans on the car horn and makes me jump.

Maya: I better go. Jack's getting edgy.
Alex: Do you want me to come with you to the airport?
Maya: No. It's probably better you don't make an appearance until I find out why he's here. I'll keep you posted.
Alex: OK. I'm here if you need me. Should I be worried?
Maya: Not at all.
Alex: Whew.

I smile because I understand why both he and my mother are concerned. The last time Kevin arrived in town, I made some horrible choices. I swing open the gate, and with a look only an angry mother could conjure, I dare my son to honk the car horn one more time. He slowly retracts his hand and averts his eyes. He doesn't look up from his phone at all during the drive to the airport.

"Dad says he's waiting outside by marker twenty-two."

"I see him." I pull over as far as I can and pop the trunk open. Kevin throws his stuff in and jumps in the back seat. "Hey, buddy," he says to Jack.

"Hey," he answers with no other form of acknowledgement.

I glance at Kevin through the rear-view mirror and shrug. "How was your flight?"

"Thankfully, uneventful."

The small talk to start a conversation is painful. I'm thankful traffic is light, and we're quickly back in Dufferin County. "Where are we going?" I ask, glancing over my shoulder.

"What do you mean?"

"What hotel are you staying at? Or are you staying with friends?"

"Maya, I don't have any friends here and can't afford a hotel."

The tension in the vehicle just doubled. "So, where are you staying?" I ask nervously.

"I thought I could stay with you and Jack."

I'm so floored that I don't know how to react.

"Maya? Is that okay?"

I shake my head slightly, trying to snap out of shock. "Err. I guess. If you don't have anywhere to stay."

"I don't."

A few-minute drive feels like hours. Through my peripheral vision, I see that Jack's fists are clenched, and he's gritting his teeth so tightly that the muscle in his jaw is starting to pulse. I'm sure we're all relieved when we finally pull into the driveway. "Help your dad with his bags," I say to Jack as he tries to escape to the house quickly. "You can take them straight up to the guest bedroom."

I watch him drag the luggage up the stairs and gesture for Kevin to follow me to the kitchen.

When I turn to face him, he's already holding his hands in the air to try and stall me. "Maya, I know what you're going to say. I'm sorry. I should have asked beforehand, but I have no choice."

I take a hard stance and cross my arms in front of me. "Really?"

"Okay, so we're going to get into this already. I thought I could settle in, and we could enjoy a meal together first." he sighs. "I have a daughter."

My eyes open wide. "You have a daughter?"

"Yes. I remarried." He opens his phone and scrolls through some pictures. "Her name is Jocelyn. She's twelve."

She must have been born the year after he left us. He didn't waste any time, but then he always moved on fast forward. Anger nudges shock to the side. "Seriously? You are, just now, telling me that you have a family in British Columbia? Now it makes sense why you don't bother with your son."

"It's not like that, Maya. I love Jack. Neither of you seemed interested in having a relationship with me."

I feel like I'm losing my shit, so I start opening cupboards and banging around dishes for no reason other than I want to make a lot of noise right now. "So, why now?

Why come all this way with your mysterious circumstances to tell us about your family? Why bother?"

"I can explain."

"Oh, please, Kevin," I say harshly. "Explain."

He swallows hard and becomes humble. "Jocelyn is very sick, Maya."

"Are you fucking kidding me, Kevin?" I rage. "You give me no notice you're arriving. You tell me nothing about why you're coming. You don't even have the decency to tell me that you're expecting to stay at my house, and on top of all that, you're telling me you have a daughter. Not just a surprise daughter, but one who is sick."

He fidgets uncomfortably. "Maya, she has a rare white blood cell disorder."

Nobody wants to hear horrible news like that. I pause, trying to calm my rage. "I'm sorry, Kevin. But what does that have to do with Jack and I?" Only then it dawns on me, and my eyes open wide.

Kevin silently answers with a nod. "She needs a bone marrow donor."

"You're here to see if Jack is a match."

"If we can't find a donor who is a match, she will die."

I suddenly feel nauseous. I try to wrap my head around the whole situation. "Kevin, you haven't bothered with the boy for years. No phone calls, no visits. You can't just march in here one day and demand that he saves the child that you *do* care about."

"I'll do it," Jack says, stepping into the room.

Kevin and I turn, startled. Fear runs through my veins as I realize he was listening to the whole conversation from the hallway.

Kevin takes a deep breath. "Thank you, Jack. Thank you."

"Wait a minute!" I interrupt. "We need to talk about this. This is not something we're just going to jump into. You still need my consent."

"Actually, Mom, I don't. We covered this in school. I don't have to be eighteen to exercise my rights in making health and medical decisions for myself."

I hold my palm on my forehead. Mostly to keep my brain from exploding out of my head. "Jack, this is all happening very fast. Let's take a minute and think about what this means."

"I'm going to take the test. If I'm a match, I'm going to do it." He turns and exits the room, dangerously leaving me alone with Kevin without any witnesses. My phone rings, distracting me from homicidal thoughts.

"Maya? Is everything okay there?" Alex asks, concerned.

"Not really. I'll explain later."

"Okay, but Jack called and asked me to pick him up. He wants to go throw the football around."

I look to the ceiling and try to rub the tension out of my neck.

"Are you okay with that?"

"Yes, he needs some space, and probably someone to talk to that isn't me at the moment."

"As long as you're okay with it, I'll pick him up in a few minutes."

"Yup."

"Are *you* okay?"

"Yes, I'm fine. Just frustrated." I look up as Jack comes bounding down the stairs and out the front door.

"Do you want me to come in when I bring him home?"

"No, but could you pick me up in the morning and take me to see my mom?"

"I can do that. My morning is free. I'm just pulling up now. He's waiting in the driveway."

"Thank you."

"No problem, he's a great kid, and I enjoy spending time with him."

"At least someone does." I glare at Kevin, who has been eavesdropping on my entire conversation.

"If you change your mind, just text me. I can be here in a few minutes."

I hang up my phone and stare at my ex-husband.

"I take it that was Alex," he says with a snide grin.

"Yes."

"I figured you'd go back to him after I left."

I raise a brow. "I don't know why you'd think that."

He laughs once, then walks towards the stairs. "I'm going to check my emails and call home. I'll stay up there out of your way."

Chapter Twelve

It was a long, restless night. In the morning I meet Alex at the end of the driveway, so he doesn't have to come into the house. The entire situation is ridiculously awkward. I'm hesitant to leave Jack alone with his father because I'm certain there will be much manipulation in my absence.

"Are you okay?" Alex asks with concern.

I grumble the entire time as I try to get situated in the passenger seat and get my seatbelt fastened. "Jack wouldn't talk to me when he got home. He just went straight to his room and closed the door."

He nods his understanding. "It's a difficult situation."

"He told you what's going on?"

"Yes, and there's something you don't know."

My head swings to look at him, and I raise my brow in anticipation. "Well? You can't stop there. You shouldn't have said anything if you weren't going to tell me."

He purses his lips. "You won't like hearing this, but try not to overreact."

Angst is already pulsing through my veins, but I know he won't proceed until I agree. "Okay, I'm ready."

"Jack knows, Jocelyn."

"What?" I furrow my brow. "How is that possible?"

"Kevin must have told her about you guys, and she reached out to Jack through social media a year ago."

I pause, trying to sort out my thoughts. "Did he know she was Kevin's daughter?"

"Yes. She didn't hide anything. She told him exactly who she was."

My hands fidget in my lap, and Alex reaches over and places his on top of them, trying to still my unrest. "So, he kept it from me."

"Yes, and he feels bad about it now, but he knows how angry you are at Kevin, and he thought you'd disapprove if you knew. In his mind, he was protecting you, though he understands now why it was not a good choice."

I try not to get emotional, but my vision blurs with the threat of tears. I blink them away. "That's why he's determined to take the test to see if he's a donor."

"Yes. I know what you're thinking, Maya. The girl didn't tell him she was sick. He found out the same way you did. There was no ulterior motive for her friendship. She just wanted to know her brother."

"Half-brother." My phone rings as Alex stops in a parking space, and I put it on speaker without looking at the display.

"Hi, Mom."

"Hey. Did you see my note? Alex and I are on our way to see Grandma. Do you want to come? We can swing back and pick you up."

"No, I just wanted to let you know that Dad and I are heading into town. I've signed the paperwork, and I'm going to do the donor tests."

I glance at Alex, then swallow hard and squeeze my eyelids closed before I answer. "Okay. If you want some moral support, wait an hour and then we can pick you up, and all go together."

"No, it's good."

I lower my head, and Alex places his hand on my neck and squeezes gently to try and relieve the tension. "Okay, we'll meet you at home. I'm not sure what's all involved in the tests, but I assume they'll take blood, so if you feel dizzy or unsteady, call us, and we'll pick you up."

"Okay. The Uber's here. Bye."

I disconnect the call but hold tightly onto my phone.

Alex tips his head to look at my face. "Hey," he says, brushing my hair behind my ear. "You did good, Mom."

Alex leans against the elevator wall and stares at me. I can feel the heat of it a few feet away. As he crosses the space in a few quick paces, I'm caught so off guard that I back up, allowing him to cage me in against the wall. His eyes lock with mine as he gets to the place inside himself where desire demands possession. His hands travel down my arms, and he tightly takes hold of my wrists. Lifting them above my head, power emanates tautly through his biceps as he pins me in place.

I feel the pressure of his body against mine with every rise and fall of my chest. When our lips meet, my body awakens with deep sensual desires. I completely lose track of my environment until the bell signals our floor and the elevator stops.

Alex turns to exit, still holding firmly onto one of my wrists. When he loosens his grip and takes my hand, I look up at him, feeling disoriented as we walk down the hall.

A ghost of a smile appears on his lips. "I want to make sure you know how I feel and what I want this time."

"Message received." I fan my face and hope my colour has faded as we reach my mom's room. It's a relief to find her sitting up and eating on her own. "Hey! Look at you! You must be feeling better."

Her hand trembles slightly, but she gets food into her mouth. "I'd feel better if this food was edible. I wouldn't feed this stuff to my cats."

I furrow my brow. "You don't have cats."

She places the spoon down on the tray. "Well, if I did, I'd feed them better than this."

Alex chuckles, and only then does she realize he's with me. Her face brightens up, and she reaches out her hand. "Alex! It's so nice to see you. If I knew you were coming, I would have freshened up." She looks at me with a look of annoyance. "Honestly, I must look a fright."

Alex takes her hand and leans in to press a gentle kiss on the top of her head. "You always look beautiful to me, so don't even give it a second thought."

She giggles like a schoolgirl. "Maya, if you don't seal the deal soon, I might just date him myself."

I'm horrified.

"I'm not entirely sure I can handle you," he says with a wink.

Kill me now. "Has the doctor been in?"

"Yes, early this morning. He said I'm stable, and there's no reason for me to stay here."

"That's wonderful news! When can I take you home?"

"I'm not going home."

"Well, of course not right away. You can come and stay with Jack and me. I'll throw Kevin out of the spare room."

"No, I'm not going to stay with you."

"Don't be ridiculous. You can't stay on your own. You're not strong enough."

"Exactly."

"I'm confused."

"You're not listening, Maya. I'm not going home. Yours or mine. The time has come." She reaches for something on the table in front of her. "I found the brochure the nice firefighter left me."

I take it out of her hand and glance at Alex. "This is for a senior's residence."

"Yes."

"Are you going there temporarily until you get stronger?"

"No. I can't manage on my own anymore. I'm going to sell my house." She turns her attention to Alex. "You can sell it quickly and get a good price, can't you?"

He looks at me nervously before answering. "Well, I think you and Maya need to talk about it a little more, but if that's what you agree is best, I'll look after it."

"Why don't you just come to stay with us? Save your money," I add.

She gives me a stoic look. "Maya, I'm not ever getting better. I'm stable for now, but I will need medical assistance, and as I get sicker, I will need more help and monitoring. I'm not going to burden you and Jack with that."

"Seriously? You're not a burden."

"You know I don't need your permission to make the best decision for me, right?"

I know I won't persuade her today, but I'm not done yet. "I suppose we could arrange a tour and ask some questions."

"I already called. I'm going tomorrow."

"You're going tomorrow? How?"

"They have a shuttle, and they said they'd come to pick me up."

My eyes open wide. Alex picks up on my silent plea for help.

"Maya, why don't you go and find out from the nurse what the plan is for discharge." He steers me toward the door. "Let me talk to her alone for a minute," he whispers.

I stand at the doorway out of her sight.

"I'm not senile," she says to Alex as he returns. "You're going to try and sweet talk me into changing my mind."

"Not at all! And I don't think I could if I tried. Now I know where your daughter got her stubbornness. We should slow down a bit. Maya would like to go with you while you tour places and decide."

"I'm not touring places. This is the place I'm supposed to be."

Alex raises a brow. "Because the firefighter told you that."

"Yes. Why doesn't anyone believe me?"

"Why would he know what's best for you? And why does he care?"

"I don't know, but if you were here, you'd understand. There's no other option. I'm just going to see what rooms are available. The doctor has already sent over all my medical requirements and charts."

"Okay, but can we let Maya take you and see for herself that this is a suitable place and their level of care is up to her standards? She loves you very much, and I don't think she believes anyone can care for you as well as she can."

I peek around the corner, trying not to be seen.

"You can come back into the room, Maya. I know you're still standing there."

I never could put one over on her. I step back into the room and give her my *special* smile. Alex looks somewhat alarmed.

"Oh, for heaven's sake, Maya," My mother scolds.

"What?"

She turns toward Alex. "She made that face in every school photo."

"That's terrifying," Alex admits.

"You guys know I can hear you, right? That's not a face. It's a smile." I say wounded.

"Her father used to say it looked like she sat on a pinecone."

"Mom!"

Alex laughs. "That's exactly what it looks like."

My head and shoulders fall in defeat.

"Stop pouting, Maya." My mom scolds. "If you must, you can take me to pick out a room tomorrow."

My phone notification goes off, and I look at it quickly. "Jack's home. I should go home and check on him."

Alex nods.

I kiss my mom on the cheek. "I'll check with the nurse about your discharge time tomorrow and pick you up. I'm not sure if I'll make it back later. I have some clients this afternoon."

"It's okay, dear. I'm just going to rest. I get exhausted in the afternoons."

Reluctantly, I leave. The weight of our conversation is starting to settle in. Alex takes a call and wanders a short distance down the hallway while the nurse gives me all the details for discharge. The sun from the courtyard window shines brightly down the corridor, making him appear almost ethereal as he turns toward me with a reassuring smile. He ends his call as I approach. "Sorry, I needed to talk to that client."

"It's okay. I feel bad I'm taking so much of your time."

"I want to be here," he assures me. "Did you get the information you need?"

"Yes. The nurse had some great things to say about the level of care at this place. She said it's the best place for her to be."

"Do you have many clients to move around tomorrow?"

"I think I should take a leave of absence. The nurse said there's no way of knowing how much time she has left."

Alex frowns. "I'm sorry."

I purse my lips, unable to respond. Understanding my need to maintain control of my emotions, he takes my hand and walks me toward the car. "I can clear my morning and go with you."

"No, I'm okay."

"Are you sure? I don't mind."

"You've done so much already. I've got this."

"Okay," he says, looking defeated.

"You can come over afterwards and bring me a treat. I think I'm going to need it."

"I can do that."

I smile. "Can you take me home? I want to check on Jack."

Suddenly and without warning, a murder of crows descends out of nowhere. I duck and dodge them as they sweep around us while we rush to the SUV.

"What was that all about?" Alex says, unnerved, as he opens the door. They dissipate as quickly as they appeared.

"Fucking birds," I mumble.

Before I can get into the vehicle, a lone attacker flies one last time overhead. A number of expletives escape from my mouth.

Alex gasps. "Did he just…"

"Yup."

"On your…"

"Head. Yes, Alex. It shit on my head."

Alex passes me a box of tissues while doing his best not to laugh aloud. He can't even look at me when I get in and buckle up. "Are you okay?" he asks, trying to compose himself.

"Yes. I need to go home and shower."

"But first, we're going to buy lottery tickets."

"Are you going to tell me you believe it's good luck if a bird craps on you?"

"Don't you? The universe is sending you a message, Maya. Be a believer."

If he only knew the half of it.

Chapter Thirteen

"When will you have the results?" I ask Jack the following day as he brushes past me to put his cereal bowl in the sink. I sigh. Yesterday, I tried to talk with him about his choices if the tests returned positive, and he shut me down with one-word answers. This morning, he still won't even look at me. How did I become the bad guy?

"They said in a couple of days. Dad says the sooner, the better."

"If you're a match, you'll have to go to British Columbia and complete the procedure there."

He gives me an annoyed look. "Yes, Mom. She's too sick to travel here. All her specialists are there."

I try not to respond emotionally. "Okay, I'm just trying to have a discussion. It's not like either of you has kept me in the loop."

"There is no loop. Just figuring it out as I go."

"Fair enough." I dry my hands on a dish towel and place it on the counter beside him. "I'm taking Grandma to see a retirement home today."

"Why would you send her to one of those places?" he snarls.

"I'm not. She made the arrangements herself. I asked her to move in with us, but she won't listen to me. Maybe you can talk some sense into her?"

"Maybe. I'll call her later."

"Thank you. I love you."

He shakes his head and exits the room to avoid my outstretched arms. "I love you too, but you're annoying sometimes."

I shrug. "Only sometimes?" I say aloud to myself. "I'll take it."

When I arrive at the hospital, my mom is sitting in a wheelchair on the curb with a volunteer and all the belongings she had with her. "Are you in a hurry?" I ask as I get out of the car. "I would have come in and got you."

"I was going crazy in that room. I needed some fresh air."

She gets to her feet, and the volunteer helps me get her in the car. She's lost so much weight that a good breeze would blow her across the parking lot like a feather. I'm acutely aware that crows are watching us from around the property.

"That's strange," the volunteer says, looking around. "I've never seen so many of them out here before." She turns and goes back inside.

My mom says something half in English and half in Irish. I have no idea what she said, but I'm sure it wasn't polite.

Montgomery Gates Retirement Living is only a few minutes through town. I pull up to the front door, and a pleasant-looking young woman awaits our arrival. "Welcome! Let me help you. I've got a wheelchair for you because you must be tired."

I glance at my mom, confident she'll refuse.

"Thank you, dear," she says as she sits.

I furrow my brow, concerned.

"No problem. Let us do all the work today."

We're only a few feet in the door, and there's a commotion in the lobby. The girl at the front desk politely tries to reason with an elderly man at the elevator. "It's working fine today," she shouts.

"Working fine," he grumbles. "It's not working fine. You need to stop hiring those young kids who know nothing. They probably learned how to fix stuff on that Google or YouTube. If I had my tools, I would fix it properly the first time."

"I know, but we're in the way here. A new resident is coming to see the building."

They turn to look at us. "Don't take the elevator," he warns as he walks toward the dining room. "It's broken."

The manager tries to hide her embarrassment. "Sorry. That's one of our residents. He used to be an elevator technician. Sometimes, this elevator has a mind of its own, and none of the service guys can figure out why."

I look at her with my eyes wide, expressing my alarm. As we step inside, she keeps explaining as the door closes and she presses the button. "Sometimes, it doesn't matter which floor you push it goes to the sixth floor, and stays there. I can assure you nobody has ever gotten stuck in it because the door always opens."

"Strange." I press my hand on the wall to see if I can pick up on any supernatural energy.

"Yes, but it's only just started happening and only a few times. We'll get it fixed; don't you worry. Nobody is in any danger."

"It seems like a death trap to me," my mother says as the door opens and she's pushed into the hallway. "Did you have a fire here? I smell smoke."

"No, no fires. I should mention that open flame burning isn't allowed because of our residents who use oxygen. Burning candles and smoking is prohibited inside."

"I don't do either, so that's fine."

The woman unlocks a door and holds it open while I manoeuvre the wheelchair through. "Wow," I look around the nearly empty room. "It's much bigger than I thought it would be."

"This is our one-bedroom apartment. There's a lot of space here. Your mom was clear that she was not interested in the studio."

Mom looks at me over her shoulder. "Who wants your bed in the same room as your television and the kitchen?"

I laugh. "Me. That sounds like a dream. No stairs, no walking, everything conveniently close."

"There's a small kitchenette with a sink, a small refrigerator, and some cupboards for storage for snacks and dishes. Rent includes three meals a day in the dining room. If she needs help, we can add a portering charge to her bill, and they'll take her there and back in her wheelchair."

"How much will that cost?" I ask reluctantly.

Before she can answer, my mother tips her head back to look at me behind her. "Never you mind. I'll do all the wheeling and dealing, thank you."

The manager notices my look of frustration and gives me a sympathetic smile. "We can review the monthly rent and any additional services you want to add later." She walks to her right and points out the bathroom at the end of a small hallway. "The bathroom with railings and a zero-transfer shower, and this is the bedroom." She directs us to the left.

I stick my head in the door. "Oh, there's a bed in here already."

"Yes, the hospital arranged for it to be sent over."

"She needs a hospital bed?"

"It's a comfort thing. It will help her adjust her position to aid in breathing and taking her medicine. Also, help her sit up if she has visitors."

"Oh, I guess that makes sense. I suppose there's a charge for that, too?"

"Yes, there's a rental fee."

All I hear in my head is CHA-CHING.

"I'm not sure what arrangements you've made to move her stuff here, but if you like, we can bring up a few pieces of furniture for the living room for a few days."

"I haven't made any arrangements for furniture."

"You can book the elevator with the front desk when you bring her stuff over. They'll reserve it for you, so you don't have to wait. You let us know what you need in the meantime."

"Thank you," my mother says, reaching out for her hand.

"You're welcome. The nurse will come up and see you shortly, and your daughter is welcome to join you for dinner tonight." She glances over at me. "Normally, we charge for guest plates, but for the first few days, please join her as much as you'd like, and we won't charge you."

I begin to feel overwhelmed, and I wish there were somewhere to sit down. "This is all happening so fast. When would she be able to move in?"

She looks at my mom, confused, and my mom looks away sheepishly. "I guess your mom didn't have a chance to tell you, but today is her official first day."

I purse my lips and hold back my honest thoughts. "I guess she didn't have time to tell me. So, you're staying here tonight?" I ask, walking around to the front of the wheelchair.

"Yes, dear."

"We're not looking at other options, and I get no say in the matter."

"None."

My eyes well up, and I struggle to blink the tears away. The manager places her hand on my arm in a consoling manner.

"I'll get Jack to help me bring over some of your stuff this afternoon."

The Irish brogue that suddenly appears in her voice soothes me somehow. "Thank you. I don't need much, just a few nighties and clothes."

"What about your medicine?"

The manager flips through some documents in a folder she's been carrying. "We have all that here. The hospital dispensed it and sent it over with instructions. We'll ensure she gets what she needs and monitor her pain levels."

My heart has a strange heaviness, like someone is squeezing it. "I'll come back later and have supper with you then."

"I don't think I feel like going down today, Maya. I'm drained. I want to get into bed and have a wee rest. Just bring me some clothes when you have time tomorrow."

"You don't want to go down for dinner?" I ask, feeling wounded.

"We can have someone bring her a tray if she wants to rest today."

"At an additional cost, I'm sure," I grumble.

She smiles. "Not today. Today, it's on the house."

"How do I get a hold of her if I need to talk to her?" Before I finish my sentence, the manager hands me a card.

"The number on the top is direct to her room, and if you can't reach her or if you need to talk to someone at reception, call the number on the bottom. The nurse and the wellness office numbers are there as well."

"Wow, you're organized."

She gently touches my arm. "It's not my first rodeo. I promise we'll take good care of her."

I nod, and the door swings open, startling me. A rather stout woman enters the room with a full cart of rattling pill bottles and medical equipment. She stops abruptly and looks at me, confused. "You're not the patient, are you?"

I laugh and stand to the side, exposing my mother to her view.

"Ah! That makes more sense. Come on," she says as she pushes the wheelchair toward the bedroom. "I've got to take your vitals and get you settled. We're going to be best friends, you and I."

"Goodbye, Mom," I holler as she disappears.

"I'll go down with you to the lobby."

"Thank you."

She pulls the door closed behind her. "I'm sure this is concerning for you. Usually, the loved ones make the arrangements and know what's going on." The elevator opens, and we step in. "I can appreciate how it feels to have your mother make all her decisions regarding her care."

"It sucks."

She hands me an envelope. "Everything we discussed with your mother is outlined here. The rent agreement and the health care provisions. She's already signed everything." We exit into the lobby, and I hold the brown manila envelope close to my chest as if it holds top-secret classified documents. "If you have any questions or concerns, please call me."

"I will. I'll be back tomorrow."

She smiles. "Just sign in at the front desk when you visit."

The minute I leave the building, I can hear the annoying cawing of a nearby crow. I constantly search for it as I hurry to the SUV and jump in. I call my sister on my way home, but she doesn't answer as usual. My brain races in a million directions, all leading to dismal thoughts. I try to keep it together, but when I see Alex parked at the end of the driveway and leaning against the trunk, waiting for me, the floodgates open, and by the time I get out of the car and into his arms, I have achieved a hard sob.

"Oh, sweetheart. I'm so sorry." He wraps me in his arms and holds me tight. "I knew I should have gone with you."

"She's staying there tonight in an empty apartment with nothing but a hospital bed that was delivered this morning. They even charged her for sheets."

"Did she know she didn't have to stay?"

"Yes, but she wanted to."

"Then there's not much you can do."

"The nurse came in before I left. She said they'll be dispensing her meds and monitoring her pain levels, and they'll do the best they can to keep her comfortable." A few more sobs delay my thoughts. "She's never told me she was in pain before all this happened. Why didn't she tell me?"

Alex strokes my hair and rocks me gently. "Because she didn't want you to worry about her."

I push back to pull the tissue out of my pocket and wipe my nose. "This is the beginning of the end, isn't it."

He squeezes me tighter. "I'm afraid so. I think she's been trying to tell you that for the past few days."

I hold my hands over my face, then gently wipe my tears away. My breathing stutters one last time as I slowly come to terms with everything. "I better pull myself together before Jack sees me."

Alex leans back so he can see my face. "There's nothing wrong with kids seeing their parents show emotion. It permits them to have feelings as well. Trust me. It would confuse Jack if you didn't show how you feel. He'd probably think you don't care. Then you'll really have a problem."

"You're right. For someone who doesn't have kids, how do you know so much?"

"I might not have kids, but I know people. It's my job. If you can't read people or know their core needs and values, you make a really shit salesman."

I laugh. "I never considered that."

He loosens his grip. "Let's make the most of this shitty day, shall we? I'm going inside to say hello to Kevin."

I gasp and shake my head. "No."

Alex smiles and waggles his eyebrows. "Oh, YES!"

"You're not going to go all caveman, are you?"

He shrugs playfully. "Maybe. It depends on Kevin."

Against my better judgment, I lead Alex into the house. Kevin jumps up from the couch when he sees him enter the room. I look at the several empty beer bottles on the coffee table and know at once I'm going to regret this decision.

Kevin reaches out his hand. "Alex. Good to see you again."

Alex gives his hand a firm shake. "Drinking this early in the afternoon? Good to see you're maintaining your great father standard, Kevin."

"Alex!" I say, regretfully.

Kevin takes a hard stance. "Well, at least I have a child. Still single, Alex?"

"No. I'm in a relationship, Kevin." He pulls me closer and anchors me to his side. I drop my head in shame.

"Can we just stop, please," I implore.

Alex looks into my eyes and nods. "Of course, sweetheart. Kevin, I'm sorry to hear about your daughter. Jack has told me all about her, and she sounds like a wonderful girl."

"She is," Kevin says, letting down his guard. "I only hope that we can find a donor. I don't know what I'd do without her. Without a donor, she won't have very long to live."

"How long did they say the results would take?"

"A few days." He looks in my direction. "I thought I'd stay, and if they're positive, I can escort Jack so he doesn't have to travel alone."

I nudge Alex to make him give me some space. "I appreciate that." He's going regardless of how I feel, so at least he won't have to travel alone for the first time.

Alex's body stiffens. "If Jack is a positive match, we'll go with him. He's not donating anything without his mom and me there," he says in an authoritative tone.

I feel my chin drop and my mouth gape open.

Kevin nods. "Of course, and you are welcome to stay at our home."

What the hell just happened? I stumble with my words. "Errr. Thank you."

"The least I can do is return the hospitality."

"Agreed," Alex says. "It's the least you can do."

I close my eyes and wait for Kevin to unleash his wrath.

"What's going on in here?" Jack asks, entering the room.

"Nothing," I answer, trying to sound nonchalant.

Jack furrows a brow suspiciously. "Well, you're all acting weird, and now I feel awkward."

Alex places his hand on Jack's shoulder. "No worries, Bud. We're just talking over optional travel plans if your results are positive."

Jack looks between us, trying to work out if that's the truth. "Okay, but has someone worked out the dinner plans? I'm starving."

"Yes," I jump into action, relieved by the break in tension. "I'll go start dinner right now. Alex can help me."

"Are you sure you need my help?" Alex asks with a ghost of a smile on his face. "I could stay here and keep Kevin company."

"Oh, hell no." I grab his arm and drag him behind me until he follows me without resistance.

"I was just being hospitable," he says insincerely when we reach the kitchen.

I try not to laugh. "You made your point. He's a douche. I know it, you know it...hell, even Kevin knows it."

Alex nods his understanding of where I'm going with this. "Jack is his son. I get it. I'll show him respect around him."

"Thank you."

"Just so you know, I'm staying tonight."

"You can hang out as long as you want."

"Oh, no." He pulls me in close. "I'm staying the night."

Chapter Fourteen

The sun is barely rising, and I'm wide awake, thinking about the awkward silence over dinner. The darkness fades, unveiling Alex's muscled body beside me. Filtered light uncovers his face as if a mask has been lifted. Even as a teenager, I always found him ruggedly handsome. It's hard to believe he could improve with age, but the years have treated him well.

I wasn't sure letting him stay was a good idea, but when I became restless in the night, his kisses silenced my thoughts and calmed my mind. I'm feeling chilly since he's stolen all the blankets, so I wiggle closer, tugging on the blanket and trying to coax him to wrap his warm, comforting body around mine.

Even in his sleep, he's in tune with my needs. Without opening his eyes, he lifts the edge of the blanket and pulls me toward him. I can feel his warm breath on my neck as he anchors me against his body, and his hand caresses from my hip to shoulder and then settles on my breast. He lets out a sleepy groan as his hand cups me and firmly squeezes before brushing his thumb across my taut nipple.

He gently rocks his hips, rubbing against the crease at the top of my bottom. With each gentle thrust, his cock gets harder until it's fully erect and hard to ignore. My woman parts twitch with excitement, and I respond by pushing back against each stroke. His warm breath turns to playful nibbling. The firm caress of his hand is now firmly tugging on my nipple. I let a small groan of pleasure escape, signalling a green light for him. His hand slides down my body, hooking my panties and sliding them down. I squirm as he reaches between my thighs and brushes across my sensitive clit. Alex growls and forces my legs apart, gaining full access to what he desires. Friction and pressure push me back against his hard cock, my excitement making it easy for its generous length to slide between my legs from behind. Stimulation coming from both sides has me panting in anticipation.

I don't even realize I'm moaning until Alex gently places his hand over my mouth and whispers in my ear. "Keep the purring quiet, kitten. There are too many people in the house."

I nod, and he moves his hand back to my breast to continue with hard tugs and firm pinches. I swear he's trying to make me call out. "Please," I whisper.

"Please, what?"

"Don't make me wait any longer."

"I thought I'd make you cum like this today."

"No. Alex, please."

"Say my name again. I want you to say my name and acknowledge it's me who is bringing you pleasure."

"Please, Alex. I need you inside me."

He grabs my hip and forces me onto my back. I'm a dripping, twitching mess of sensitive nerves that needs release. On strong arms, he hovers over me, teasing me.

There's no need to guide him. The first thrust finds the way, and with each following stroke, I struggle not to call out or moan with pleasure. I'm fixated on nothing but the slow and steady rhythm. Heels firmly planted, I tilt my hips and widen my knees, ensuring there is no space between us. Tightening around him with every forward motion, I circle my hips and find the pressure I need, creating waves of pleasure growing in strength. Alex nears his breaking point, and as I reach mine, we climax together with an incredible force. The final few thrusts make the headboard of the bed bang against the wall with his release.

As our bodies become still and we pause, trying to catch our breath, I suddenly have an alarming thought. "Do you think Kevin heard us?"

"I hope he did." Alex rolls gently to the side and pulls me into his arms.

"That's not cool," I scold. "If you're going to make love to me, it should be about me...not Kevin."

He releases his grip and sits on the side of the bed. "Believe me, Maya. He wasn't on my mind at all until you said his name."

"I'm sorry. Don't leave. This whole situation is just really weird. I'm having trouble navigating my thoughts and emotions."

He turns and leans in to kiss me. "I'm not leaving. I'm going to have a shower; somebody made a mess."

I smile. "It wasn't me."

"It was definitely you. Seriously, we might have to hire a lifeguard."

"That's disgusting." I hear the shower turn on, and I stretch my neck to watch his magnificent body get under the warm spray of water.

"You better come join me," he hollers. "We have to get your mom sorted out today."

I walk to the doorway and watch for a few minutes as he scrubs bubbles over his body. "Here," I offer, taking the scrubby out of his hand. "Let me get your back."

He turns without objection, and I take my time tracing and scrubbing every inch of his muscular body. I think about what happened a few moments ago, and arousal comes over me again. I pause, and he turns curiously to see what's wrong. "I think you better finish this yourself or turn up the cold water."

Alex smiles and hands me the body wash. "I'm done. I'll get dressed and meet you downstairs since you can't seem to control yourself."

"Good plan." I firmly push him out of the shower. "Towels are hanging on the back of the door."

I reach for the cold water faucet and turn it up. He says something from the other room, but it's only mumbling to me as I stand directly under the shower head and immerse myself in thoughts of anything other than Alex. It doesn't take long before my thoughts are about my mom. That's a topic to block any sensual thoughts and arousal.

Alex has coffee ready by the time I get downstairs. Kevin is on the phone on the back deck, and Alex answers my unasked question. "It's his wife, calling with an update on his daughter."

"Oh." I frown. "I know he's a jerk, but watching your child go through that must be hard."

"Yeah, I felt a little sorry for him this morning. I even made him breakfast."

I raise a brow.

"I think he knows that you're mine. I can cut him a little slack."

"I'm yours?"

He pulls me into his arms. "Mmhmm. Is there any doubt after this morning?"

"None at all. I was yours after the awards banquet."

He kisses my lips with a victorious smile. "You looked amazing in that dress."

"We'll have to go out somewhere fancy again sometime."

"Deal. Hey, I wanted to ask you something. Have you ever wondered why Kevin isn't donating bone marrow? You'd think he would be a match."

"I never thought of it, honestly. Do you know something you're not telling me?"

"It was something Jack mentioned. Something Jocelyn confided in him. He didn't come right out and say it."

"But?"

"I feel like Jack is concerned for her well-being for reasons other than just her health."

"What do you think is going on?"

"I don't know for sure, but have you noticed Kevin sniffles a lot for a guy who doesn't have a cold? And why does he look twenty years older than he is and has no money?"

I turn to watch Kevin through the window, processing Alex's theory. Now I know why he is dead set against Jack travelling there alone.

Alex pulls me into his arms. "Never mind, maybe I'm just reading too much into things. I'd rather talk about us." He presses his lips against mine.

"Good morning," Jack chirps as he enters the room.

"Good morning!" Alex replies as if we weren't just smooching. "I left you a plate of breakfast on the counter."

"Sweet!"

"Sorry," I say as Jack passes me.

"Sorry for what?"

"That you walked in and saw…"

"You and Alex kissing?"

My face turns beat red. "Yes."

He shrugs. "That doesn't bother me. It's been so long since you were in a relationship that I was beginning to wonder if you were into girls or something."

"Nope." Alex grins. "She's not into girls."

"Stop it!" I warn.

Jack spreads jam on his toast. "I can tell. You might want to line your headboard with bubble wrap."

My life is over. I turn and stomp out of the room.

"Where are you going?" Jack asks.

"I'm going to wait in the car."

"Maybe we should ease up on her a little bit." I hear Alex say as I reach the hall.

"Nah, where's the fun in that?"

I slam the door behind me, the force of it nearly launching me off the top step. The neighbour across the road is hosing off his driveway, and he looks up when he hears the noise. Embarrassed, I wave and smile. "Hi, Henry."

"Everything okay over there?"

"Sure, everything's fine. I tripped over Jack's shoes on the way out the door."

He nods, but I know he doesn't believe me. By the time they come outside, I've had time to cool off and find a little humour in it. Jack and Alex get into the car as if nothing has transpired. Obviously, I'm overreacting again.

"What's the goal today? Are we moving stuff over there?" Alex asks.

"No, I rented a truck for the weekend. I'm trying to get a hold of my brother and sisters to get their help."

"Good luck with that," Jack says from the back seat.

"Can I just stop by the house and get some small things today? Some personal items, clothes, a fold-up chair, and a small table for her to put beside her bed."

"Of course."

I feel anxious when we pull up to the house. By the time Alex stops in the driveway, I'm feeling lightheaded.

"Maya?"

"Huh?"

"Are you okay?"

"Yeah." I reach for the handle and get out.

Jack is right behind me. "I'll go water the garden and then meet you inside."

"Great. Thank you."

I push open the front door, and a cold, eerie feeling washes over me. It's only been a short time, but it feels like it has been uninhabited for a hundred years. Cold and quiet, the darkness makes me feel edgy. Alex turns on the light and draws the curtain. The movement forces dust particles to float through the air, making me feel like we've entered an abandoned home.

I walk from room to room, taking inventory of what's there and handing Alex items I think we can take today. He starts a pile at the front door. I open her bedroom door and still see her lying on the floor. I jump when Alex places his hand on my shoulder.

"I think the small suitcase she uses when she stays over is in the closet. I'll throw some things in there for her."

Alex finds it and opens it on the bed. I rummage through each drawer, one at a time, and pick up a few of everything I think she'll need. She'll want to have clothes to wear down to the dining room.

"What can I help with now?"

"Could you pack up the TV and the remote? And something to put it on, I guess."

"Of course."

"Do you think we have room to take this bedside table?"

"Lots of room." He picks it up and carries it to the front door. "I'll tape the remote to the back of the TV."

"I have no idea where you'd find the tape."

He laughs. "I brought a roll of mover's tape with me. I carry it with me in the car."

I sit on the end of the bed, feeling ultimately defeated. I can hear Alex and Jack talking as they go in and out, loading things into the car.

Alex startles me as he enters the room a few moments later. "Are you almost done in here?"

I get to my feet. "Yes, I guess so." I pick up the picture of my mom and dad on their wedding anniversary and place it inside the suitcase. "It was Mom's favourite picture. It should be there."

"Agreed. Jack grabbed a couple of plates, utensils, and snacks from the cupboard. I'm not sure if they're for her or him."

"Likely for him. Once she's settled, I can take her grocery shopping and get food she can nibble on if she doesn't feel up to eating in the dining room."

It seems like a very long drive to the other side of town. The truth is, I'm dreading it. I want to warn Jack about what he's about to walk into, but as he constantly reminds me, he's not a child anymore. I think he knows what to expect.

The girl at the front desk brings us a trolley to use to take stuff up to Mom's room. I wait in the lobby while the boys unload the SUV. Within minutes, there's a commotion at the elevator again. The same elderly man stands in the doorway, forcing it to stay open and causing the alarm to go off. I can see from the front desk that he has a small toolbox that looks more suitable for fishing tackle than tools. Jack and Alex return and look at me to gauge the seriousness of the situation.

"He was here the other day, too. I think he might have dementia. They say he's harmless."

"He was an elevator technician before he retired. When you're finished signing in, I'll get the situation under control," the girl at the front desk assures us.

A small crowd gathers as they return after lunch.

"Get out of the elevator. You're going to make me miss my show." One of the residents says to him, poking him in the shin with her cane.

"It's broken." He insists.

Another woman speaks up. "It's not broken. Everybody knows it's haunted. Claudia saw the ghost of a firefighter in there the other day."

Now they have my attention. Alex leans in and whispers in my ear. "Ghost of a firefighter?"

"I heard."

"Strange coincidence, no?"

"That's no ghost," the man argues. "That's my son visiting me, you crazy old goat."

"Oh boy." The young girl at the front desk peeks around the corner into the offices behind her. "I'm going to need some help." Several people emerge from their offices in seconds and professionally diffuse the situation.

"Is it always like this?" Jack asks the pretty young volunteer at the desk.

"Not at all. It's usually quite boring. I'm not sure why there's suddenly so much excitement around the elevator."

Alex gives her a charming grin. "Hell hath no fury like a woman delayed from watching her afternoon game shows."

"Very true," The older brunette giggles as she returns to the desk.

I feel a little jealous for a moment, and I wouldn't say I like it.

"Come on, beautiful," Alex says, sensing my insecurity. "Now the crowd has cleared, let's go see your mom."

I watch Jack's reaction as he steps into the elevator. I can't sort my energies out these days, but he'll know if something haunts this elevator. I wait, but he gives me no clues. "Sense anything on this elevator?" I finally ask.

He leans his head to look at me around Alex. "No."

"Really? I'm sure lots of people die here. Nothing?"

"No!" he says, annoyed. "Do you sense any dead people?"

"No. My spirit radar has been on the fritz."

Alex raises a brow. "Is there something I should know about you two?"

I laugh as the door opens. "Sometimes we have *feelings*. My mom always says the magic of Ireland flows through our veins. It's a gift."

"Are we talking Long Island Medium or Voodoo Master?" he asks, concerned.

"Neither," Jack answers. "It's more like a heightened intuitive awareness. Sensing energy and emotion. Sometimes from the past."

"Oh," Alex says, relieved. "That, I understand."

"That's exactly what I said," I protest.

Jack shakes his head and rolls his eyes as he pushes the trolley down the hallway. "That's not what you said at all. What you said made us sound crazy."

I make a face behind him, and Alex tries to hide a smile.

I knock and try the door handle. It's unlocked, so I open it and peek in. "Hello, it's Maya. We're just going to let ourselves in."

There's no answer, so I push the door open and hold it while Jack pushes the trolley in. "Let me go and make sure she's decent before you come in to say hello."

She looks still, propped up in the hospital bed and slumped to the side. "Mom. It's Maya. Jack and Alex are here too."

She opens her eyes and tries to lift her head.

"Jack wants to come in and say hello. Is that okay?"

"Yes, of course. I was sleeping. I think they're giving me too much medicine. All I want to do is sleep."

I wave Jack into the room.

"Hi, Grandma."

"Hello, Jack. I'm sorry, I must look a fright."

"Don't sweat it, Grams. You look fine."

160

"Sorry to interrupt," Alex says from the doorway. "I'm just wondering if you want the television in the bedroom or the other room. I'll start setting it up."

"Hi, Alex! Could you put it in here, dear? I haven't got the strength yet to go out to the other room."

"Of course. Where would be the best spot?"

She looks confused as if he suddenly started speaking a different language, and she doesn't understand a word he said.

"Mom?" I prompt. "On which side of the room would you like him to set it up?"

"Over there is fine," she says, pointing.

"I'll get right on it."

She returns her attention to Jack. "I hear you have a sister."

Jack turns to look at me, and I shake my head. "I didn't tell her a thing."

"No, she didn't tell me; your grandfather did. He visits me and gets me caught up on the news."

This is not a good sign if ghosts are coming to visit her. "I'll be right back. I need to get something." I'm only a foot out of the room when I hear her giggle.

"Your grandfather doesn't come to visit. I overheard her on the phone when she thought I was asleep."

"Grandma!"

"Don't spoil my fun," she warns.

Now I know where Jack gets it from. I bring the suitcase into the room and hang up some outfits. "I'll just put the nighties and other things on this shelf in the cupboard until we bring you over a dresser or something."

"That's fine, dear."

"What else do you want me to bring over here?"

"Nothing."

"You don't want me to bring your stuff here?"

"No."

"So, I'll just leave everything at the house in case you go back there?"

"No. I told you Alex is going to sell the house."

Alex looks up from where he's sitting on the floor, hooking up the television cables.

"Do you want me to store everything at my house until you've thought about it?"

"No, Maya. I no longer have use for anything. It's just stuff. Get rid of it."

"But I've rented a truck."

Alex gets to his feet and turns on the television. "There you go."

"Perfect. Thank you."

He hands her the remote. "I have an idea. What if we brought some stuff here so it doesn't look so empty and we have somewhere to sit when we visit? Some stuff we can leave at the house because it's better if it's not empty when we list it for sale."

She waves her hand, showing indifference. "You decide. I'm too tired to care anymore."

He frowns. "Maya and I will decide what to bring here, but you need to think if there's anything you want to go to someone specific so we can make sure they get it."

"I will."

I use the opportunity to tell her something I previously felt selfish asking for. "Mom, there's a few keepsakes from Ireland that I'd like to have."

"I don't own anything of value, but you go ahead and take whatever is special to you. I want you to have those things."

"Thanks, Mom."

"I've been watering your garden," Jack adds.

She reaches for his hand. "You're such a good boy. Have you met the cute little blonde girl that volunteers around here?" She closes her eyes, and we realize she's fallen asleep, so we quietly leave the room and let her get some rest.

When the elevator arrives, Alex pushes the button for the lobby. The door closes, and the elevator goes up. I raise my brows. When it stops on the top floor, the door opens. Jack sticks his head out and looks down both halls. He shrugs as the door closes. "Nobody there."

Suddenly, we both have the same thoughts. "Didn't you tell me the same thing happened at the hospital?" Alex asks.

My body tingles. "It must be a coincidence, right?"

Jack leans against the back wall. "Well, the hospital elevator went up to a floor that didn't exist, so there's that difference."

"What?" Alex says, concerned.

The door opens in the lobby, and we all hurry out, causing people to stop and stare. Alex leans down and whispers between us. "They probably think somebody passed gas in there."

I stop dead in my tracks and look at him. Then at Jack. I shake my head at how much they're alike. "You two have been spending too much time together."

Jack is the first one to speak on the drive home. "If Grandma is going to sell her house, can we dig up some of the flowers from her garden and plant them at our house?"

"You can," Alex says, looking at him in the rearview mirror. "But you should do it before we list it so nobody complains that we've taken or moved things after the fact."

"I love that idea, Jack." I turn to look at Alex. "How will we organize all this if we have to go to British Columbia?"

"Let's not worry about it until we know for sure. I can do the listing and have an associate oversee any viewings while we're away."

"I guess we'll know in a day or two," Jack says from the back seat. "They said they'll call me either way."

Kevin is sitting out front when we pull into the driveway. I can see from the car that he's struggling and appears to have been crying.

"Do you want me to stay?" Alex asks, concerned.

"No, it's all good. I'll call you if I need you."

Jack delays getting out of the vehicle, and when he thinks I'm out of earshot, I hear him ask Alex a question.

"Will you come with us to B.C. if we go?"

"Of course, bud. Unless you don't want me to go."

"I do," he responds, sounding relieved. "I mean, if you can leave work without getting in trouble."

"It's one of the perks of working for yourself, kiddo. I can make my own rules. But I have friends in the industry who will help if I need them to, so I'm free to travel with you."

"That's good."

"Are you worried?"

"A little. But not for me. I'm worried about Mom. I think it would be great if you were there to support her. I don't think she's coping very well."

Alex nods. "I've got your back, buddy."

I sit beside Kevin on the step. Now I can tell his eyes are red from something other than crying. "Everything okay?"

He sniffs several times. "She's not doing so good. I feel terrible being away at a time like this."

"Can I ask why you and your wife aren't a match for your daughter?"

"We both were. Unfortunately, we both have things in our health history that made us ineligible."

I don't ask because I suspect I know what those things are. "It must be terrifying." I put my arm around him and squeeze him. "Hopefully, they won't prolong the results, and we can get her healthy and back on her feet soon."

Chapter Fifteen

The last two days flew by quickly. I watch from the family room window as an old friend, Ben, and his brother, Jake, load the last few things into the back of their truck. I'm blessed to have friends who are always there for me, even if I don't talk to them every day. Alex and Jack are meeting them at Montgomery Gates to help them unload.

My phone rings, and I grit my teeth as I answer it. "Hi, June. I've been trying to get a hold of you."

"I've been busy."

"I needed to talk to you about Mom. She's not doing well."

"She called the other day. It sounds like moving her was the right call."

"You know?"

"Yes."

"And you couldn't call me to let me know. Or even offer to help?"

"As I said, I'm busy. Did you ever think maybe nobody calls you because you're so dramatic?"

Rage flashes through my body. "Dramatic? Do you realize your mother is going to die? At any time."

"We're all going to die eventually."

I blink my eyes rapidly, trying to understand her nonchalant response. "I could have used your help today. Are you planning on going to see her soon?"

"Of course, just because I don't overreact like you doesn't mean I don't care. She is my mother too, after all."

"Really? Because lately, I feel like I'm an only child."

"You always had a connection with her that she didn't have with the rest of us."

"Maybe it's because none of you put any effort into a relationship with her."

"We all do our best, Maya. It's not for you to judge. I have to go."

She hangs up before I can sort out my thoughts and voice them aloud. Probably for the best.

I pull the door closed behind me, pausing a moment before I lock it. The loud hammering behind me makes me jump. I slowly walk down the path to where Alex is putting the *'for sale'* sign on the front lawn. He gives me a sympathetic smile as I hand him the extra keys.

"Where's Jack?"

"He went with the boys to get food, and then they'll drop him off at home. I figured you'd be okay with that. It's not like they're strangers."

"I'm totally fine with that."

"Do you want notice to approve times when someone requests a showing?"

"Just let me know when someone will be here so I don't show up."

I rub the back of my neck, trying to relieve the tension there. The past few weeks have been exhausting, both physically and emotionally.

"I'll do everything I can to sell it with a quick closing."

"I appreciate it. She paid her first and last month's rent from what was left of her savings. I can't afford to pay more than a month out of pocket for her room."

"I understand." He pauses, and there's an awkward moment where I'm afraid I've made a mistake opening myself up and letting people in. He wraps his arms around me, and he smells so good that I have to force myself to pull away from the temptation.

His hands linger on my arms. "Maya, what can I do?"

"Find a cure in time."

He frowns. "Do you want me to follow you to your place?"

I need to put some distance between us for now. "No. I'll call you tomorrow."

Looking wounded, he watches me walk to my car and stands perfectly erect next to the sign with his picture, waiting for me to leave. I wave once as I pull away from the curb. I'm sure he's still watching me as I come to the stop sign at the end of the road, and I'm not entirely sure why I'm feeling this way. It's as if I've absorbed all the emotional energy I'm capable of, and there's no more room in the tank.

Instead of taking my usual route, I take a quick left and head into town. As much as I'd like to go straight home and catch up on much-needed sleep, I'll stop and check in on my mother first. I'll rest sounder knowing that she's having a better day. I wish I had the support of my three siblings, but after what June said, I finally understand why they've left me to tend to her affairs.

I check in at the front desk before going to her room in case anything requires my attention. I'm glad the woman on duty was the one who helped us the day we moved in. She was kind and patient, and very helpful. "How was her day?"

She gives me a consoling smile. "She didn't feel like leaving her room today."

I frown.

"Moving day brings a lot of anxiety and excitement, and she's still experiencing a few side effects from the new medication."

"Was she at least a little *less difficult* today?" I ask hopefully.

Her expression lightens. "She didn't throw her dessert at anyone today."

I furrow my brow, feeling embarrassed. "I'm so sorry about that."

She smiles, trying to put me at ease. "The past few days have brought some overwhelming changes. At least we know she doesn't like butterscotch pudding."

I close my eyes and caress the tension at my temple. "Thank you for understanding."

I take the elevator to the fifth floor and find her door slightly ajar. She's sitting, hunched over, in a wheelchair in the middle of the room. Her eyes are closed, but I'm glad she's dressed and out of bed.

"Hi, Mom." I look around the room at the contents of her house. It makes her apartment feel cozier and more familiar.

She lifts her head and gives me a vacant look.

"Have you had dinner yet?" I ask, concerned.

"I'm not hungry."

"You have to eat. You need to keep your strength up."

"Why is all my furniture here?"

My brows form a hard line. "You asked Alex to sell the house, remember?"

"It's my house. I've lived there for sixty years."

My expression softens. "I know, Mom." I watch as she takes a tissue out of her pocket and wipes her nose with a shaky hand. "Let's go for a walk and get some fresh air." I position myself behind the wheelchair and grasp the handles. I'm met with some resistance as I try to push. "Mom, lift your feet, please. We're going to get out of the room for a little bit." I clench my jaw and wait. "Mom!" I close my eyes and take a slow, calming breath.

There's a tense moment as we power struggle before she reluctantly lifts her feet so I can navigate the doorway and push her into the hall. Her room is right next to the elevator, and as soon as I press the button, the door opens, and the gentleman from the elevator scandal is waiting inside. A dark-haired man moves to let us in, and I can see the resemblance to the elderly man beside him. His son, the firefighter, I assume.

"Sorry," I apologize for my less-than-perfect wheelchair steering as I pilot my mother into the corner.

The elderly man gives me a polite smile. "It's easier if you back them in," he advises with a thick Scottish brogue.

"Ah, rookie mistake," I admit.

"But then, sometimes you have to try and turn them again to back them out."

I sigh.

"You'll get the hang of it," the younger man encourages.

I hope she's around long enough, so I do. I get a heavy, dismal feeling as frigid air surrounds me. I glance up at his kind face and nod toward my mother. "Someone's been a naughty girl, so a little time in the corner is probably appropriate."

"I heard she's not a fan of pudding."

I look at him, horrified.

"The floors are as thin as the walls," he explains. "Sometimes the residents are a lot like children. They tell it the way it is and have no filter." He glances toward his father. "Most of them have earned the right to speak their minds." The elderly gentleman stares at the light panel on the wall, and his expression becomes vacant; distant. It's as if the rest of us in the elevator ceased to exist.

"There's no excuse for her being rude," I add.

My mother looks over her shoulder at me and gives me an inquisitive look. "Who are you talking to?"

"I'm Ryan. This is my father, Earl."

Before I can introduce us, the door opens on the main floor, and the elderly man steps out without acknowledging us. He's greeted by one of the employees, who takes his arm and escorts him into the dining room. I wait for his son to follow, but he motions me to go first. I back my mother out and thank him as I push her toward the patio door. She shelters her eyes from the late-day sun hanging low on the horizon. I find a vacant sitting area and turn her away from the glare. Sitting beside her, I try to smile.

"How are you feeling today?"

"Terrible."

"I figured that since you haven't commented on the two young, handsome men I sent over with your stuff this afternoon. Ben and Jake?"

"I noticed, but I'm just too tired to care."

I sigh. "Is the new medication not helping?"

"It makes me feel fuzzy."

I nod. "But does it take the pain away?"

"I guess so. I can't stay awake long enough to tell."

"Its job is to make you more comfortable and help with the pain. When you're tired, you need to sleep. Your body needs rest. You need to listen to what your body is telling you."

"It's telling me my room feels like an igloo."

"I'll go by the house and get you some sweaters. Is there anything else you need?"

"I need to go home."

Emotions build up inside me, and it's all I can do to stop the eruption. My frustration is noticeable in my tone. "This isn't easy for me either, Mom. This was your choice. You wouldn't even discuss other options with me. Why did you insist on coming here if you don't want to be here?"

"I came here to die."

Hearing her speak the truth stings, but it's a reality we can't change. She's going to die. We don't know how much time she has left. Guilt weighs heavily on me. I want to push her into the parking lot and take her back to my house, where loved ones surround her. The only thing stopping me is knowing I can't give her the care she needs at home. Feeling at a loss for how to comfort her, I take my sweater off and drape it over her shoulders to keep her warm and take her back inside.

As I pass through the dining room, Ryan signals for my attention.

"She's asleep," he advises as I stop. "Be careful she doesn't fall out."

I look around her hunched body and acknowledge his concern. "Thank you." The staff member from the front desk greets me at the elevator and offers to see she gets safely into bed. I reluctantly allow them, feeling like it's my responsibility. "Goodnight, Mom." I kiss her on the top of the head and leave her in caring hands.

I call Alex on my way home.

"Hey."

"Hi."

"I thought I would have heard from you earlier."

"I stopped by to see my mom."

"Is she feeling more at home with her stuff there?"

"On the contrary. She asked me why it was there and said she needed to come home. Did she seem confused when you were there?"

"She didn't talk to us much. They had her up out of bed, but she didn't seem to be herself."

"She's not herself."

"I'm sorry, sweetheart. I can pick up something from the bakery and meet you at the house."

I need him, right now. I need his strength and support. I need him to hold me so tight that all the pieces of me that are starting to break are held together. And yet, I find myself bricking those needs behind a wall. "Actually, Alex. I'm just going to go home and get some sleep. I'm exhausted."

There's a pause in which I know he's using the time to talk himself out of pressuring me into accepting his company. "Okay, but if you need me, call me. I don't care what time it is. I'll come by."

"Thanks,"

"Maya."

"Yes."

"Are you okay? You don't seem much like yourself either today."

"I'm just tired."

"Okay. Get some rest."

A single tear streams down my cheek. I don't know why I lied to him. I only know the way I'm going to survive this is to find the strength within myself. People can't be trusted to stick around.

Chapter Sixteen

My phone rings bright and early on Sunday morning.

"Alex?" I ask sleepily.

"I'm sorry to wake you, but something is happening at your mom's house. I just drove by, and there were people parked in the driveway, so I stopped. Maya, it's your sisters."

"What the fuck?"

"They're inside the house now."

I bolt upright and sit on the side of the bed.

"They brought a trailer."

I jump to my feet and knock everything off my nightstand. "I'm on my way. Funny how they can't find time to come and visit with our mother, but when there's stuff up for grabs, they found time in their schedules."

"I'll wait for you outside. Take your time and drive carefully. I'm parked behind the trailer, so they can't leave until I move."

I twist my hair into a bun, secure it to the top of my head, and then grab a sweatshirt. "I'm leaving now."

Kevin and Jack are sitting eating cereal at the kitchen table. "Where are you going in such a panic?" Kevin asks.

"Alex just called. Apparently, my sisters just arrived at my mom's house with a trailer, and if I know them as well as I think I do, they're planning on cleaning her out of everything valuable."

Jack's chair screeches across the floor as he gets to his feet. "I'm coming with you."

"So am I," Kevin says.

I grab my keys from the hall table. "It's okay. I can handle this."

"No, you can't," Jack insists. "You need reinforcements."

They push past me, not waiting for my approval. I exhale harshly, knowing it's against my better judgment.

When we arrive, a few furniture items are already loaded onto the trailer. Alex leans against his car with his legs crossed at the ankle. He chuckles as I pass. "I see you wore your formal pyjama bottoms to the party."

"No time to change," I growl, heading to the door.

"Don't kill anybody," he advises as I rush past him. "Maya!"

I turn to look at him as I continue to walk.

"Don't take too long; someone just booked a time to come see the house. They'll be here in an hour."

"Should we follow her in?" Kevin asks Alex as he approaches.

"Let's wait out here until we hear screams and the sound of chaos."

Jack raises his brow. "Do you think it'll get that bad?"

Alex shrugs. "Have you met your mother?"

I turn as I reach the door and give him an angry look before entering. Jack looks terrified.

Hearing voices in the bedroom, I wait in the hallway with my arms crossed. The door swings open, and as my sister locks eyes with me, she gasps and drops the armful of goods she's carrying.

"Maya!" she says awkwardly.

I hear a thump from the room, and June appears shortly after. I'm so aggravated. "What are you doing here?"

"Mom said we could help ourselves to whatever we wanted."

"So, you're happy to let me do all the work and handle all the details, but you wouldn't ask me if there was anything here that I would like to have before you take everything?"

"Oh, well, is there anything you want?"

"I want *you* out of this house."

"Okay, you're angry. But since we're here, we'll take some things with us. Then you don't have to get rid of everything by yourself."

"Are you kidding me? Are you going to make it look like you're here to help me out? Have you ever gone by to see her? She's only five minutes up the road."

"Oh," Jennifer says, "Unfortunately, I have plans this afternoon."

"I have to get home to take the kids to gymnastics," June adds.

"So, you show up, grab as much stuff as you can for your financial gain, and you don't even plan on saying thank you or a final goodbye to your mother?"

They look at each other, neither of them offering excuses.

"Has anyone even spoken to Brian yet? Does he know she's dying?"

"He knows," Jennifer answers. "I spoke to him a few days ago. He's on vacation out on the West Coast for the month. He said he didn't want anything from the house, so he had no reason to return early. He'll wait for the money."

Anger consumes me, and I begin to see red. "Some days, it amazes me that I'm related to the rest of you." I place my hand on my forehead. "Get out!"

Nervously, they head toward the door. "You can take what you've already got on the trailer, but you get nothing else until she's gone. As executor of the estate, I will disperse whatever is left how I see fit."

June stomps out of the house, cursing. Jennifer tries to smooth things over. "I'm sorry for blindsiding you, Maya. It was all June's fault. She convinced me that you wouldn't mind."

"You know I'm not buying any of that, right?" I escort her to the front door.

"You're right. We're assholes."

I nod, enthusiastically.

"Before we go, could I ask you about one thing?"

"Hurry up. People are coming to see the house shortly."

"I was looking through her jewelry for a ring but couldn't find it."

"What ring?"

"It was gold and had the Irish hands symbol and crown."

"It's called a Claddagh Ring."

"Right, well, it had a green, emerald heart and some diamonds on the band."

"That's her wedding ring, Jennifer."

"Do you know where it is?"

I'm stunned. "It's on her finger, for fucks sake." I push her the rest of the way out the door. "She's not dead yet."

The boys jump into Alex's SUV when we appear out the front door. He rolls down the window as I approach. "Are you okay with them taking the things on the trailer?"

"Yes, they can have them."

He moves his vehicle as I walk to the window of my sister's truck. "Give me the house key," I demand.

"You're overreacting again, Maya," June says through the closed window.

I purse my lips. "You know what? Keep it. I'll change the locks before you have time to return anyway. And just so you know, Alex has the house under video security, so don't get any stupid ideas because the next time you show up, I'm sending the cops instead of coming myself."

"Let's go," Jennifer says nervously.

"We have just as much right to the stuff as you do, Maya," June says as she backs out of the driveway.

"No. No, you don't. You have no rights. You have a hell of a lot of nerve but absolutely no rights."

She flips me the bird as she drives away. "Oh, that's mature. Go visit your dying mother, you selfish twat!" I suddenly realize several neighbours are nervously watching on. I give them an apologetic wave. When Alex pulls back into the driveway, they are laughing. I cross my arms. "What's so funny?"

Nobody answers, but they're still chuckling. I sigh. "None of that better appear on TikTok." The snickering continues. "JACK!"

"I promise," he finally answers.

I glare at Kevin in the passenger seat. "Don't look at me. I don't even have TikTok," he says defensively.

"Me neither," Alex confesses.

"It better not show up on social media of any kind," I warn.

"Yes, ma'am"

Jack leans forward between the seats. "While we're here, do we have time to dig up some roses to take home?"

"I forgot about that."

Alex looks at his watch. "If we do it quickly. They will be here in about half an hour."

I follow Alex to the back gate. "They don't look very healthy at all," he says as he enters the yard. "I'll grab some pots and the shovel from the shed."

It's strange, but it seems my mother became sick, and the roses stopped thriving.

"Maybe the magic will return once we take them home and replant them," Jack says optimistically.

I didn't think Jack believed. "Which ones should we take?"

"I think we should take at least one of each kind."

"Of course," Alex says as he returns.

A crow sits on the fence and watches. I realize how ridiculous I'm being, but I refuse to make eye contact with it. Its cawing is loud and annoying.

"A friend of yours?" Alex asks, noticing my avoidance.

"I'm going to go out front to make a call," Kevin says, leaving us to do all the work.

Alex and Jack exchange glances, then carefully dig out a selection of each plant.

"Are you guys okay to take these home and replant them? I want to go visit my mom for a little while."

"Of course. You go. I'll let you know if I get feedback from the viewing today."

I break off a few healthier-looking blooms and wet the tissues in my pocket with the garden hose. Wrapping the dampened cloth around the fragile stems reminds me of how fragile her life is right now. It won't erase the nagging knowledge that this is the beginning of the end, but their beauty may give her some comfort and enjoyment for a day or two. One last look at the withering roses as I make my way to the car breaks my heart.

It's expected these days for her to barely acknowledge me when I arrive. I search the room for something to hold water and settle on an extra-large, paper take-out cup that I dig out of the trash. I place it on the windowsill and stand back to admire them. "Well, it's not a fine crystal vase, but they smell pretty."

She manages a small smile, and the flicker of brightness in her eyes is the closest I've seen to happiness in weeks. "Coffee grinds are good for roses. I'm not so sure about brewed coffee."

My phone rings. "It's Alex. I'll call him back."

"You like him," she says, smiling.

"Alex?"

"You should ask him to marry you."

I laugh once. "And why would I do that?"

"You two have unfinished business."

I pause. "That sounds rather portentous."

"Honestly, Maya, stop being so old-fashioned. It's okay for the girl to ask these days."

"Why would I ever want to get married again?"

She frowns. "I don't want you to be alone after I'm gone."

My heart aches. "Don't worry about that, Mom. I won't be alone. I have Jack."

She narrows her eyes. "The dog? He was hit by a car twenty years ago."

I raise my brow and then remind myself she's taking some powerful meds. "No, Mom. My son, Jackson. The dog's name was Jasper." Her eyes glaze over, and I can already tell I will get whiplash from the subject changes today. "I'm going to eat lunch with that Earl character today."

"Oh? The one that wants to fix the elevator?"

"He's an okay fella for a Scot." She frowns as she turns her attention to the wilted cuttings in the coffee cup. "What will happen to the roses in my garden?"

My heart is shattered, but I try not to show it. "They'll stay at the house, and the new owner will enjoy them."

She reaches for my hand and squeezes it tightly. "They're dying too, aren't they?"

"Not if I can help it, but I've never had your green thumb."

"I can feel their life force fading. Like we're somehow connected."

That imagery haunts me all the way home. Alex calls again, and this time, I answer.

"Hey."

"Hey, is this a bad time?"

"No, I'm just on my way home."

"I've got some feedback on the showing. I could tell you about it at lunch."

"Lunch?" I look down at my clothes. "I'm still wearing my pyjamas."

"It's Sunday. I won't judge."

"I haven't even had time to grocery shop," I say, trying to buy myself time to devise an excuse to turn him down.

"It's all good. I spoke with Jack, and he and I will fire up the barbecue. I've got steaks, and he's wrapping potatoes in foil. Kevin is making a salad, if you can believe that."

My heart feels heavy. Never in a million years would I think I'd be sharing a meal with my ex-husband AND my ex-boyfriend. "I was going to run in, do a few things, and then go back to see my mom after dinner. She's having a bad day. Have you already planned it?"

"We did. And Jack has to eat anyway, so you don't need to worry about that. You can relax, and we'll do all the work. Then I can tell you what the other agent said."

I don't think I'm going to persuade him otherwise. "Okay, if you insist. I'll see you there."

"I insist."

I hang up the phone and feel like there's a tremendous weight pushing down on me. I pull into the driveway and sit in my car. It's too much. It's…just…too…much. My heart races, and I feel lightheaded. Panic washes over me and takes hold of reality, forcing it into unreachable existence for what seems like an eternity.

"Mom!" Jack yells. "What's wrong with her?" he asks Alex.

"I think she's having an anxiety attack. She'll be okay." Real life starts to tune back in as Alex opens the car door. "Maya? Sweetheart, are you okay?" He caresses my cheek and strokes my hair. "Let's go in the house." He gently coaxes me out of the car and supports me until I get my legs under me.

"I'm okay," I assure them. "I was just a little overwhelmed for a minute."

"On second thought..." He opens the gate to the yard and walks me in. "Come sit outside and get some fresh air while we finish making lunch."

Jack pulls a chair into the shade on the deck and insists I sit. "There's no way you're going back to visit Grandma today. I'll go to check on her instead."

"It's okay, Jack. I can go."

"Absolutely not. You need a night off."

I look to Alex for support, but he shrugs. "Are you ready for the feedback on the house?"

"Sure."

"These buyers have been looking in the area for quite some time. As soon as they saw the listing, they jumped on it. Their agent said they liked the location, but the house was older and would require a fair amount of updating."

"We listed at a price that accounted for that, right?"

"Yes, but it's a young couple who have been shut out of the market because they can't compete with the bidding wars going on right now."

"So, this is a good chance for them."

"It is."

"But?"

"When an agent leads with a list of all the things that are wrong with the property that will cost their buyer money, it usually means they're going to come in with an offer much lower than asking."

"It's already listed as low as I'm willing to go."

"I understand. We need to get your mom as much money as we can to cover her care."

"For however long she needs it."

He busies himself with the steaks on the grill. "Grab me a plate," he says to Jack. "These are ready."

He turns to meet my impatient stare. "Sorry, Maya. I don't mean to add to your stress. A few more people have booked viewings. It will be fine."

Alex and Jack work hard to keep the conversation pleasant and light during lunch. The negative energy I've been absorbing the past few days catches up with me, and I can't fight it anymore. After Jack leaves to visit my mom, Kevin washes up the dishes, leaving Alex and me alone in the family room.

I yawn. "Well, sorry to kick you out, but I'm exhausted."

"Kick me out?" he asks, confused. "I was going to stay."

"Not tonight, Alex."

The muscle in his jaw tightens, and his demeanour becomes dark and moody. "Walk me to the car."

I slip on my shoes and walk down the driveway with him. He stops and leans back against the door. "What's going on, Maya?"

"Nothing," I say, trying to avoid an emotional relapse. "I'm just tired."

"It feels like you're pushing me away."

"What? No. There's just so much going on."

"I know, and we were handling it together. Supporting each other. Now Kevin is here, and it doesn't feel like you're interested in having me around."

I can't find words.

"Do you still love him? Has something rekindled between you?"

His accusations shock me. "No! Nothing like that. I don't have feelings for Kevin anymore. Not in many years."

"What is it then?"

"I don't know." I avert my eyes.

"Do you love me, Maya?"

"Alex."

"No, don't try to avoid the question. Do you love me? Because I love you. I never stopped loving you."

"But you let me go."

He reaches for my hands and reels me in closer. "I'm not going to let you go ever again. I was young. I didn't know."

I fight the tears as he anchors me against his chest.

"I don't want to lose you again. I'll leave tonight because you asked me to, but I won't let you push me away this time." He kisses me on the top of the head and releases me. "We can talk it through tomorrow, okay?"

"Okay."

He leans in and kisses my lips. I feel the way I did the very first time he kissed me. I was as scared and confused then as I am tonight. "Goodnight, get some rest."

"I will. Call me tomorrow."

"You're the first thing I think about when I wake up."

I walk to the house, swatting at mosquitoes and thinking about the words I have waited seventeen years to hear. Alex Thomas loves me.

I close the door and kick off my shoes when I feel eyes on me. I look up to find my ex-husband leaning against the kitchen door jamb with a tea towel over his shoulder and a snide smile.

"Trouble in lovers' paradise?" he asks with a grin.

I stomp halfway up the stairs, then stop and march back down. He stands erect when he sees me. "Screw you, Kevin. And your stupid salad."

I turn and rush up the stairs and then slam my bedroom door behind me. I flop on the bed and laugh at my absurd, immature insult. I think about how hurt Alex looked tonight, and my heart squeezes tightly. I pick up my phone and flip through some of the pictures of us during the past few weeks. Pictures of us together enjoying life. Pictures of him and Jack doing guy stuff together. As fate would have it, they have an awful lot in common. We're both lucky to have him in our lives.

There's not much I can do about the hurt and mistakes in the past. But I can avoid the same mistakes in the future. I dial his number.

"Hey," he says in a sullen tone.

"Hi. I love you, too. Please come back."

Chapter Seventeen

I wake the following day feeling unburdened by past baggage. I get out of bed, leaving Alex asleep.

There's something I need to do, and I can't avoid dealing with it any longer. I pull into the driveway of the home I grew up in as a child. Today, it looks tired...worn. The gate to the backyard is open, but I know I won't find my mother tending to her roses.

I take a deep breath and unfold the piece of paper I've been carrying in my pocket for two days. I can't keep putting it off. I unlock the door and flip on the lights as I walk through the house. It feels empty and clinical. I can't imagine how it would feel had I let my sisters take everything they wanted.

I unzip a small duffle bag and leave it open on the only furniture left in the room. After taking a deep breath, I search the closet for the items my mother wishes to be buried in and place them in the bag. There are no words to describe the emotion I'm feeling at this moment. This is one of those things in life you're never prepared for until you have to do it.

On my way out, I grab the bottle of her favourite country roses skin lotion from the bathroom counter and tuck it into the top of the bag.

Alex calls as I toss the bag into the passenger seat.

"Where'd you go?"

"I had something to get from my mom's house."

"Why didn't you wake me up?"

"You looked so peaceful, and I figured you had to be worn out."

"I am, but I had to shower and get ready to go into the office anyway. I have good news. I have an offer on the house."

"Already?"

"Yes, I met with their agent a few minutes ago. What's your availability?"

"I'm on my way to Montgomery Gates to have lunch with Mom, and you can meet us there."

"That works for me."

"Perfect. Give me half an hour, then meet us in the dining room on the main floor."

When I arrive, I overhear two young volunteers whispering about how the fire alarm keeps going off on the sixth floor. "I hate going to that floor. It's creepy."

They smile politely and continue to whisper as I pass.

"How was she at breakfast this morning?" I ask the girl at the front desk as I sign in.

"She's having a good day. We even saw her smile."

"That's great news."

I get into the elevator and push the button for the fifth floor. I close my eyes and curse when it passes my floor and goes to floor six. The door opens, and standing in front of me is Earl. "Hi! Are you getting in?" I ask, placing my hand on the door to stop it from closing.

"No, I forgot something. I have to go back."

"Okay," I say, stepping out.

"Where are you going?" he asks confused.

"I was going to get Gladys on the fifth floor, but the elevator didn't stop."

"It's broken, you know."

"I know."

"They won't let me fix it."

"Well, you know they can't. The union won't let them."

He opens his door, and I see a sudden glimpse of understanding on his face. "That makes sense."

"I'm going to take the stairs down one floor. I'll see you in the dining room later."

The stairwell is cold and dark. Every step echoes eerily through the corridor. I hurry to get out of there. Relieved to be on the fifth floor, I knock once and then push open her door. "Hello!"

"Hi, Maya," she answers cheerfully.

My heart is happy to see her looking more like herself today. "Guess what?"

"I hate guessing. Just tell me." She scolds.

I laugh as I slide the duffle bag out of view. I don't want to spoil a good day with that business. "Alex is coming to bring us an offer on the house. So, let's pretty ourselves up a little." I push her wheelchair into the bathroom. She sits and stares at the mirror as I run the brush gently through her silver locks. I try not to focus on how frail she's become. I've watched her age twenty years in the past week. I'm not ready for her to go. I need her. My son needs his grandmother. Does it make me selfish to want her to fight? I lay the brush down and smile. "There, now you're ready to go down for lunch."

She pushes up her sleeve and scratches at her arm. "It's so dry in here."

"That reminds me. I brought your hand cream." I grab it out of the duffle bag and twist the lid. After squirting a little in my hand, I caress it gently into her dry skin. The air fills with the fragrance of roses. "I'd forgotten how nice it smells."

"Not as nice as my garden when it blooms."

"Agreed. There!" I exclaim, feeling proud of myself. "You look beautiful!"

"You know, Maya. I'm feeling a little bit hungry today."

"Well, today is turning out to be a wonderful day."

Alex is already sitting at a table when we get to the dining room. He immediately gets to his feet when we approach. He's all decked out in a business suit and wearing expensive cologne. It's hard to stop my mind from wandering to inappropriate places. His eyes sparkle, and his smile grows wide when he sees me. I've always had difficulty protecting myself from his charm, so I'm glad I've given in. It was exhausting trying to fight it. "You look handsome today."

"Thank you."

"Did you get all dressed up just for us?"

He grins. "I'll say yes if it gets me brownie points, but this is my normal Monday morning, *a man has gotta work to pay the bills*, attire."

I shake my head. "You should have just stuck with *yes.*"

"I figured, but someone kept me awake all night, so I'm a little tired and not thinking defensively."

He moves a chair out of the way so I can push Mom's wheelchair up to the table. When she's situated, he places some documents in front of her.

He pulls out a chair for me. "It's a pretty good offer," he says, pleased.

Earl shuffles past us and sits at the table by the window. His son loyally follows and sits by his side. As Alex explains the paperwork to my mom, I look over his shoulder and give Ryan a quick wave. He nods and smiles.

Alex raises a brow and looks behind him. "Who are you waving to?"

"Earl and his son, Ryan."

"The firefighter?"

"Yeah, we met him the other day."

Alex turns in his seat. "He's not here now."

"What?" I lean to look around him and see Earl sitting alone. "That's odd. I didn't see him leave. He must have gotten a call."

My mom stares at the document in front of her. "What do you think, Maya?"

I glance at Alex, trying to read him. "I think an offer at the asking price is great."

Alex agrees. "It's always an option to turn it down and wait and see if anyone else will offer more money. It's only been on the market a few days."

"Is this the young couple that's been trying to buy their first home?" I ask curiously.

"It is. And I was saying before, I expected them to come in with a much lower offer."

"It's up to you, Mom, but I feel we should help this young couple start their lives together in their own home."

"Your father and I lived with his parents for years before we could afford our own home. Women didn't work in those days because they stayed home to look after the children. We tried to buy a few times, but the bank always turned us down because having a large mortgage on one salary was too risky. Back then, houses were only thirty thousand dollars. His parents finally helped us out with a downpayment. I remember the day your father and I moved into that house. It was brand new, and we were so excited. If Alex feels it's a fair price, I'd like to give them a chance to feel that same pride and excitement."

"They're paying what we've asked for with no conditions other than a house inspection, and they're already pre-approved on the financing. I think it's a fair deal." He takes his pen out of his jacket pocket. "Let's sign it and make someone's day!"

There are a million places to sign and initial on an offer to purchase. My mom nibbles on her lunch as Alex goes through everything and shows her where to sign. Finally, we're done.

"I'll walk you out." I leave Mom alone to eat her salmon sandwich and walk with Alex to the front door.

He turns to look at me with content. "She looks better."

"She's having a good day. I have to keep reminding myself she's never going to get better."

"It's good to see her in better spirits."

Alex reaches out and gently touches my elbow, then runs his hand down my arm and grips my hand. "I'm sorry I have to ask you this right now, but do you have power of attorney? In case anything *sudden* should happen with her health."

"I do."

"And if she…" His eyes darken with sorrow.

"I'm the only executor of the estate."

I let my guard down when he pulls me into his chest and wraps his arms around me in a firm hug. I've been strong for so many years on my own, and I'm finally okay with allowing him to protect me.

When I return to the dining room, Ryan sits with my mom at the table. I glance at the empty table beside us.

"Where did you disappear to earlier?"

"I had something to do."

"Where's your dad?"

"He went back up to his room to watch *Wheel of Fortune*. I thought I'd stay and keep your mom company."

"That's kind of you."

"I like your mom. She has a special energy." He stares at her, and a small smile forms on his lips. "She also smells like roses."

"It's her hand lotion. Roses are her favourite flowers. She grows them in the gardens all around the house."

"It reminds me of someone I used to know. Someone I loved."

"Used to?" I ask, sensing his melancholy as his smile fades. "What happened?"

"I waited too long to tell her how I felt, and she fell in love with someone else."

There's a long, silent pause before I glance to the door where Alex was standing and try to hide my current vulnerability. "Are you finished eating, Mom?"

"Yes." She drops a crumpled napkin onto the table. "I'm exhausted. Can we go back to the room?"

"Of course."

She's asleep before we reach the elevator. I look at Ryan, concerned. "Do you smell that?"

"What?"

"It smells smoky. Like something smouldering."

He shrugs. "I'm afraid I don't smell it." He pushes the elevator button. "He really does love you."

I furrow my brow, confused.

"The guy that was just here. He loves you. I'm glad he didn't wait too long to tell you."

"He got it in there just under the wire."

"I'm curious. Why didn't you marry him?"

"It's complicated." I give him a mischievous grin as the elevator door opens. I push my mom in, waking her as I jam the wheels against the transfer plate. I turn the chair around to face the front and press the button to hold the door open, but he doesn't join us. I stick my head out and look around, but he's disappeared. "Strange."

"What?" she asks, confused.

"He's gone."

"Who?"

"Ryan. The guy I was talking to."

"I'm the one taking all the drugs," my mother says, looking up at me. "But lately, I think you've lost your mind."

Kevin is sitting on the front porch looking distraught when I get home. "What's going on?"

"I'm going out of my mind. I called the lab today, and they told me the results were inconclusive. We need to go back and do them again. She can't afford any more delays."

I sit beside him. "I'm sorry."

"I'm sorry. I haven't even considered how you're doing. How is your mom, by the way?"

"Today was good, but there's no way of knowing how many she has left."

"Is there nothing they can do?"

"Make her comfortable until it's time."

Alex pulls up and jumps out of his car. "Hey! It's a done deal," he says excitedly. He pauses and looks between us. "What's going on? Did you get the results back?"

"I called today, but something went wrong, and we have to go back in the morning and give another sample."

"I'm sorry, man."

"Thanks, I appreciate it. I want to get home and see my little girl. I'm afraid she will leave us before I get there."

"Don't even put that out there into the universe." I stand up and reach out my hand. "Come on—enough negative thoughts for today. Alex has a box from the bakery in the car. Let's make a pot of coffee and celebrate selling the house."

"How did you know?" Alex asks, perplexed.

"Are you kidding me? You can't hide the smell of freshly baked cinnamon rolls. We're celebrating!"

It doesn't take long before the bakery boxes are empty, and everyone suffers from a sugar overload. Kevin stands at the door at the back of the family room, watching Alex and Jack play video games. Their usual competitiveness gets rowdy and loud. I bring Kevin a cup of coffee. "Thank you."

"I figure by the time you get used to this time zone, you'll be heading back to the west coast."

"That's what usually happens." He sips it slowly. "There's a lot of smack talk going on in there."

"Yeah, it's all in good fun, though. These two have become really good friends."

"I can see that."

"He's a good kid."

"Are you talking about Alex?"

"Ha! Very funny."

"I thought it was."

"I was thinking Jack should spend time with you so you and your family can get to know him better. Maybe sometime during the summer and alternating holidays? He only has one more year left of high school, and then he'll be adulting full-time. Who knows when either one of us will get time with him."

"I would welcome the opportunity."

"We'll figure it out then. Right now, I'm exhausted, and I'm heading to bed."

Alex shuts off the lights and climbs in beside me. He reaches for me and tries to tug me into him, but I anchor myself to the side of my bed.

"Hey," he says playfully. "What's going on?"

"Did you bring any bubble wrap?" I ask, looking over my shoulder.

"Noooooooo."

"Well, stay on your side of the bed, then."

I snicker, and Alex grabs me and rolls me over forcefully. I squeal until I'm lying on top of him. "What were you saying about staying on my side?"

"Technically, I suppose you're still on your side. I'm the one out of bounds."

"I didn't see a flag on the play."

"No?"

"No. If there was a foul, the referee missed it."

I lower my lips to his.

Alex growls as he skims his hands across my bottom and squeezes both cheeks firmly. "Be careful what you start."

I slide to the side and lay beside him. "Has Jack ever mentioned college to you?"

"What? Where'd that come from?" He rolls to his side and props his head up in his hand.

"He won't talk to me about what his plans are when he finishes school. I've tried to mention careers I think he'd be good at to try and get him thinking about college courses he needs to take, but it doesn't seem to be going anywhere."

"Maybe he doesn't know yet."

"Is that normal? I mean, I always knew the direction I was going after school. I didn't decide exactly what I would specialize in until I had done some prerequisites and figured out what I enjoyed. He doesn't seem to have any clue, and I'm afraid he's going to land on the whole *take a year off thing*, and I'm not cool with that."

"I wouldn't worry, Maya. I did a few different things before I landed on real estate."

"So, you're saying it's a guy thing?"

"No, I'm saying maybe he hasn't found anything that sounds interesting or challenging enough. I'll talk to him."

"Thank you."

"Is there any chance you'd like to reward me for my assistance?"

"None."

"Just thought I'd ask."

I roll to face the opposite direction, but he follows. "What are you doing?"

"Nothing," he says with innocence.

I feel the warmth of his body against mine as his hand gently caresses my side. I feel my body relax beneath his touch, and then he plays dirty. He gently sweeps aside my hair and presses his lips against my bare shoulder. It's only a few butterfly kisses strategically placed, but I instantly feel my lady parts twitch.

"Damn you. That's not fair."

"It's only illegal if the referee sees it," he says with a low feral tone. He seduces me with an alternating attack of gentle suction and passionate nibbling. The heat of his mouth from my shoulder to the base of my neck renders me captive to his desire.

As he makes love to me, the pressure building inside me is unbearably intimate and exciting. It's a feeling I've only experienced once before, a very long time ago, and that too, was with Alex.

Chapter Eighteen

Kevin and Jack left early for the laboratory. Alex let me sleep in since he felt guilty about keeping me awake most of the night. I make it to Montgomery Gates in time to have lunch. I'm pleasantly surprised to find out my mom is already downstairs in the dining room. I kiss her on the cheek and sit down beside her.

"It's great to see you up and around, Mom. Did you finally have a good night's sleep?"

"I did, but I'm getting tired now."

"Why didn't you go upstairs then?"

"This is where she left me."

I raise my brow. "Who?"

"Jennifer."

"My sister, Jennifer?"

"Yes."

"She came to visit you?"

"Yes, she came for breakfast."

"For breakfast?"

"Yes, she was asking about some of my jewelry."

Anger starts to pump through my veins, and I become tense. "Why?"

"She was afraid that I sold it."

A million things are running through my head right now. None of them are very nice things to say about my sister.

"I told her, anything I wasn't taking with me the day I'm buried, I'm leaving to you."

I purse my lips. "I bet that didn't go over well."

"That's why I'm stranded here."

I roll my eyes. "I'm sorry. Did she at least eat with you first?"

She looks around the room, then down at the table. "I don't think so. I don't remember eating."

I'm about to suggest we get something and take it back up to the room when I see Ryan and his father, Earl, get off the elevator. I get to my feet and smile. "Would you like to join us, Earl?"

He stops shuffling and stares at me. "He couldn't find his hearing aids this morning," Ryan explains.

"Please join us," I say louder and motion toward the table.

He hesitates and looks over at his usual table at the window. "We'd enjoy your company," I add.

He sits beside my mom, and a heavy feeling settles around me. I pull the cuff of my sleeves down over my wrists to get rid of the goosebumps.

"Are you okay?" Ryan asks, concerned.

"It just got frigid in here."

Earl and my mom share a look.

"What floor do you live on, Earl? My mom asks.

"On the sixth floor, right beside the elevator."

"Right above you," Ryan adds. "Only one floor up."

"Is that the top floor?" my mother asks.

Earl watches my mother struggle trying to open her menu with shaky hands. He reaches over and unfolds it for her. "Aye, it is."

"I heard the nurses talking the other day. They said the sixth floor is haunted."

"Well," I say, opening my eyes wide. "I imagine more than a few residents have passed while they lived here. I suppose it's possible." I turn to Ryan and tilt my head to the side. "IF you believe in that sort of thing."

Ryan scratches his head and then breaks into an amused smile. "I've never seen any ghosts wandering around up there, but that elevator does some strange things sometimes."

"There's no such thing as ghosts," Earl adds. "I'd know if my room was haunted."

The waitress walks toward the table, and Ryan gets to his feet. "I've got to run some errands. I'll be back later."

I wonder why he never actually eats a meal here. I narrow my eyes suspiciously.

"Food allergies," he explains. "It's safer if I eat at home. But I'll be back later."

It's amazing that he always knows what I'm thinking, even when I say nothing. As he exits the dining room, Alex appears. His smile brightens the room. I stand as he joins us, and he gives me a quick hug before he sits.

"What are you doing here?"

"I have a listing with one of the other residents here. I just came to go over some things and saw you hanging out."

"You just missed Ryan."

Alex turns to look toward the lobby. "Really? I didn't pass anyone."

"Join us," my mother offers. "This is Earl. He lives on the sixth floor, right above me."

"Nice to officially meet you, Earl." He shakes his hand before he sits and pulls his chair in, intentionally resting his thigh against mine. The warmth from his body radiates up my leg and begins to heat me. I put my hands in my lap, hoping they'll start to thaw. Alex reaches for my hand under the table and squeezes it. My face flushes.

"Who's this guy?" Earl asks my mother.

"He's the real estate guy."

"Are they married?"

"I don't think he's even asked her for a proper date yet."

My eyes open wide, and my face turns red. "Mom!"

"Why haven't you asked her out?" Earl inquires.

I lower my head and cover my face with my hands.

Alex chuckles and leans toward Earl. "Honestly, I'm afraid she'll turn me down."

"Why would she turn you down? You seem like a nice fellow," Earl says quite loudly.

"Oh, for the love of. . ." I raise my head to find all three of them staring at me.

"Well?" my mother asks. "Are you going to turn him down?"

Suddenly, I find humour in it and start to laugh. Alex grins and holds his hands up, waiting for an answer. "Well?"

"Can we talk about it another time?"

He looks at Earl and raises his brow. "Hey! That wasn't a NO!"

"It was definitely not a NO," Earl agrees.

Alex's brown eyes light up as he turns his attention back to me. "I like my chances."

Something catches my attention, and I see Ryan watching from the lobby. I lean to look around Alex and almost fall off my chair. His hand brushes across my breast when he reaches out to steady me.

"Look at that!" Earl exclaims with his thick Scottish brogue. "You've already gotten to second base!"

I like this man's sense of humour. "Yes, he did. And it's the most action I've seen in years."

"I said go out with him," my mother says, shaking her head in a disapproving manner. "Not put out on the first date."

I sit, speechless, while my face turns crimson red. Alex does his best to hold in his amusement. I shrug. "I've got no comeback. Time to take everyone back to their apartments."

I get to my feet and begin to pull back the wheelchair. "Where are we going?" my mother asks, looking up at me.

Earl nudges me gently to the side and takes the handles. "We're being sent to our rooms."

"Oh, for heaven's sake. Young people are so sensitive."

Alex gives me a boyish grin, and there's no point in trying to resist his charm. As we arrive in the lobby, he pushes the elevator button and pauses. "I'll come by later?"

I smile. "Sure. I'll be home in about an hour."

He reaches out for Earl's hand. "Sir. Thank you for helping me wear her down."

"My pleasure. I used to be quite the lady's man in my day."

"I suspect you still are."

I walk Alex to the door, and on the way back, I hear one of the employees at the front desk complaining about smelling smoke.

"Is there a fire?" I ask, alarmed. "I could smell it earlier."

"We've checked everything and can't find any reason to be concerned."

The young employee looks pale and unnerved. "We smell smoke all the time on the sixth floor. And the fire alarm goes off in room six-fifteen all the time, with no explanation. We changed the batteries every few days before we finally just bought a new one."

That's Earl's room. "Did it stop?" I ask curiously.

They both shake their head.

"I could smell it in the lobby just now," the other staff member continues. "It's a damp, smoky smell…like when you douse a bonfire to put it out. It's very creepy."

"I hope you figure it out." The elevator door opens, and Earl begins to back my mom in. I rush to help, but he's already navigated the space, and the door is starting to close.

I place my hand on the door to stop it from closing. "Were you going to leave without me?"

"You were busy talking," my mother says.

"Really?" I say, flustered. "You couldn't wait two minutes?"

"Never mind her, Earl," my mother says, looking up at him. "She's sexually frustrated."

"I think maybe she's just too picky."

"Definitely," my mother agrees. "Back in my day, nobody was perfect. If you couldn't attract a handsome man, you settled for one who was handy."

"The real estate guy was handsome. What's wrong with him?"

I lower my head in frustration. "You know I can hear you, right? I'm standing right here!"

It isn't until we get to her room and I help her get ready for bed that I notice she's not wearing her wedding ring. "Mom? Do you know where your wedding ring is?"

"My wedding ring?" Her appearance and slightly slurred speech indicate that her medications are kicking in. She looks at her finger, perplexed.

"Please tell me you didn't give it to Jennifer."

Her head begins to bob as it becomes heavy under the influence of her medication. "Lay back and rest. I'll look for it." I check the bathroom and the night table. I even check the pocket on the side of her wheelchair. It's nowhere to be found. I growl in frustration.

She opens her eyes. "Don't be upset, Maya. It's just jewelry. It doesn't mean anything."

"The ring and the vows you shared with Dad mean *everything* to me. I hope she didn't convince you to give it away."

She mumbles something incomprehensible as her eyes flutter open and then close again. I sigh. "Get some sleep, Mom. I love you."

Chapter Nineteen

The following day, Jack goes with me to visit. I use the opportunity of having him captive in the car for several minutes to my advantage. It's hard sometimes to pin him down and talk.

"She's had a couple of great days. She's made friends with one of the other residents and is really enjoying his company."

"His?"

"The elevator guy. His name is Earl."

He holds his hand in the air. "Stop! I don't want to know any more about it. It's my grandma."

I grin. "Did everything go okay with the retesting at the lab yesterday?"

"I guess so. They couldn't tell us what went wrong with the original results or why it took so long. Kevin lost his shit."

"That's Dad, to you."

He rolls his eyes. "I don't know why I should call him that. He's practically a stranger."

"You need to show him a little respect."

He groans. "Fine. *Dad* lost his shit."

I bite my tongue.

"They took extra vials of blood this time. I don't know why. The manager was so apologetic about the screw-up that she promised to expedite the results this time. She said they will try and have them as early as today."

"I bet he was happy to hear that."

"It's hard to tell what makes Kevin happy."

I give up. "Are you nervous?"

"Not really. Should I be?"

"No. You've done your research, and you know the possible risks for both you and Jocelyn."

"Where's Alex today?"

"He has a bunch of open houses to attend. He said he'd catch up with us sometime this afternoon. Don't forget you promised to keep up with your schoolwork if I cut you some slack on attending classes."

"I know. I talked to my teachers, and they've given me the assignments to work on. I promise I won't get behind."

"I trust you."

Jack winces as we enter the lobby.

"What's going on?" I ask loudly so the girl at the front desk can hear me over the music.

"A little lunch hour entertainment in the dining room. I think your mom is over there."

"You call that entertaining?" Jack asks the pretty blonde volunteer as he signs himself in.

"Not me personally, but there are a lot of smiles in that room."

214

"What kind of music is this?" he asks as we navigate the crowd.

"Music from their era. Most of the people were born in the forties."

"The eighteen forties?"

I see Ryan on the other side of the room and approach him. "You're such a smart ass. You must get that from your father."

"I doubt it. While Kevin has proven himself to be an ass, we have never established that he's smart."

I stop in my tracks, intending to give my son another talking to about respect. But he has a point, so I carry on.

"I see Grandma," he says, dragging me toward her. "Grams, quick, save me from this music. My ears are about to bleed."

The music stops, and Jack gives an exaggerated sigh of relief.

"Who is this young man?" Earl asks.

"This is my grandson, Jack. He has no appreciation for good music."

"No, he doesn't," Earl says quite loudly. "And his mother is sexually frustrated, I heard."

"Yes, that's true," my mother says as if it's a typical conversation to have with people.

Everyone in the room is looking at me. Jack's eyes open wide, and he gives me a traumatized look.

"Welcome to my world."

"Do you know what we should do, Gladys? We should go downstairs and play billiards."

"There's a pool table here?" Jack asks with excitement.

"Yes, in the basement."

"Can we check it out?"

I shrug. "I don't see why not."

"The elevator has no problem going one floor down," Earl adds.

"Good to know."

Jack's excitement shows when we step off the elevator on the lower level. "There's a putting green and air hockey!"

"There's also a bar."

Earl insists on pushing my mom down the long hallway. "On Thursday nights, we have happy hour and play bingo here."

"That sounds like fun."

"I suppose so. I got a bingo, but all they gave me as a prize was a chocolate bar. Not even the kind I like."

"That's unfortunate," Jack says as we enter the room. "I'll rack 'em up."

I'm not sure if this is possible from the position of a wheelchair. "Are you playing, Mom?"

"Of course, I'm playing. I'm not missing out on all the fun."

"I didn't know you played pool, Grams."

"I used to play all the time with your grandfather, but that was a long time ago."

She struggles but gives it her best effort. I'm not sure how I can help. "Are you able to stand to take your shot, Mom? Maybe it's because you're sitting too low."

"These cues are too long for me. Your father bought me a child-size cue once. It was better for me."

Jack whips out his phone. "We can take care of that, Grams."

"What did you just do?" I ask suspiciously.

"Ordered her a youth cue on Amazon. It will be delivered tomorrow."

"That's fast," My mom says, amazed.

"This isn't the eighteen-forties anymore, Grams," he leans in and talks into her ear as if he's whispering, but everyone can hear. "And I ordered you the pink one."

"Oh!" she says delightedly. "That's my favourite colour."

"I know! Tell me the truth. I'm the best grandson you've ever had, right?"

"You're the only grandson that ever visits," I mumble to him under my breath. "So, Earl. Where's your son?"

"My son, Ryan?"

"Yes."

"He's gone."

I wait for him to expand, but he continues to play without any further explanation. I glance over at Jack, who shrugs.

My mom is having a wonderful time, but she's starting to look tired. "We should head upstairs. Alex will be here soon, and I think it might be time for your medication, Mom.”

“I’m tired of taking so much medication,” she grumbles.

“Me too,” Earl adds. “Some days, I rattle like a pack of TicTacs.”

We take the elevator up to the lobby.

“I wonder what’s for dinner today?”

Earl points at the menu taped to the elevator wall. “It’s the same thing every day.”

“I don’t want that again. Can’t we order a pizza?”

I consider it. “I don’t see why not, but won’t it upset your stomach?”

“Probably, but it might be the last time I ever get to have pizza.”

The girl at the desk looks up. “Could you tell the nurse to bring my mom’s afternoon medication to the dining room?”

“Of course.”

“Is it okay if we order food and sit in there?”

“No problem at all. But there’s a private dining area just around the corner that isn’t currently booked. You could eat in there if you like.”

“Sounds fancy, thanks!”

I texted Alex, and twenty minutes later, he arrived with pizza.

I greet him with a grateful kiss.

"Why is she kissing the pizza delivery guy?" Earl asks, confused.

I try not to laugh as Alex places the pizza boxes on the table.

"That's not the pizza guy," my mom corrects. "That's Alex."

"Who's Alex?"

"The love of her life."

"Oh, I remember… the one that got away. I thought the pizza guy looked a lot like the real estate guy."

"Alex *is* the real estate guy. I'll probably have to remind you again tomorrow."

Jack hangs on every word. "This is much more fun than Mr. Carver's math class."

"You need to do well in math, my boy. You'll need it to become an elevator technician," Earl says.

"I wasn't aware I would become an elevator technician, sir."

"Of course you are. What else would you be? I was the best elevator mechanic there ever was. I could diagnose a problem with my eyes closed."

"That's wonderful. I bet they don't make them like you anymore."

"No, they don't. And I'm going to pass everything I know on to you. Tomorrow, you bring your tools and report to me."

Jack's eyes widen, and he looks at me in a panic. "Just go with it," I suggest.

Earl firmly places his hand on Jack's shoulder. "You'll call me Grandad from now on. We're family now. We'll look after each other." With that, he nods and moves on to the pizza.

"Made a new friend, I see," Alex says to Jack as he hands him a slice of pizza.

"I'm scared."

"Don't worry, bud. The sad thing about dementia is he probably won't remember any of this an hour from now."

One of the volunteers sticks her head in the door. "Miss Dunn?"

"Yes," both my mother and I answer simultaneously.

"Maya?"

I raise my hand while trying to gnaw through the stringy cheese on my slice of pepperoni.

"There's someone here looking for you. Kevin."

"Oh, you can send him in to join us. It's okay."

I look up when he enters the room and stands there silently, watching us while tightly clenching a folded paper in his hand.

"Hey, help yourself to some pizza. We're just hanging out today."

"Thanks, but I'm not hungry. I just came to say goodbye."

The room goes quiet. My brow creases. "Goodbye?"

"I'm heading to the airport. I'm leaving."

The tension in the room heightens as he becomes agitated.

"What's going on? Is your daughter okay?"

A notification goes off on Jack's phone, and he looks down at the screen. "We got the test results."

I look at Kevin, searching his face for any clue.

"Are you a match?" Alex asks.

It's way too quiet.

"Jack?" I persist.

"No."

"No? You're not a match?" I shake my head in disbelief. "I don't believe it."

Jack shows the results to Alex, who reads them and looks at me with confirmation.

"I don't understand. Why isn't he a match?"

Kevin walks toward me and hands me the papers he's been holding tightly. "Because he's not my son."

Shock hits me hard. "What? That's not possible."

"Look at the paper, Maya."

My hand trembles as I unfold the document. "This is a DNA report." Shock pulses through my body. "Why would you order a DNA report?"

"I didn't the first time around." He gives Alex a heated stare. "But, I've got eyes."

"Kevin," I say, feeling exasperated. "This can't be right. I wasn't with anybody else after I met you. The only person I had sex with before I met you was...."

All eyes turn to Alex. I feel like I'm going to hyperventilate. "How did I not know I was pregnant when we met?"

"Well, here we are," Kevin says impatiently.

"I always wondered," Alex admits.

"You did?" I ask, shocked.

Kevin paces impatiently. "Did you ever wonder, Maya? Did you ever wonder why I left?"

I stumble with my words. "Because we grew apart. You stopped loving me."

He shakes his head no. "Because even after we got married, I could tell you still loved him."

"That's ridiculous. I loved you. I married *you*."

He cocks his head to the side in a reflective manner. "Well, maybe a little, but admit it. There was part of you that wasn't available for me. There was a part of you that you shared only with him."

I find it hard to swallow. Could he be right? Had it been that way the whole time, and I didn't even understand it myself? My lack of response doesn't put him at ease.

"Well, Alex, you win. It wouldn't have mattered how hard I tried or how much I did. The biggest problem with my marriage was that *I'm not you*." He picks up his backpack and swings it over his shoulder. "Congratulations. It looks like you're a father, after all." He turns and leaves. I watch until he's out of sight, still trying to process what just happened.

Earl leans in and nudges my mother. "What's going on between the pizza guy and the piano player?"

"That's not the piano player. That's Kevin. Maya's ex-husband."

"Maya's ex-husband plays piano?"

She places her hand on her head. "Shhh. I'll explain it to you later."

222

I turn slowly to look at the others in the room. I don't know what to say. After a moment, I panic. "Alex. Alex, I'm sorry. I swear, I didn't know."

"It's okay," he assures me.

"Wait," Jack says, fully realizing what it means. He turns to Alex. "So…*you* are my real father."

Alex shrugs nervously. "Apparently."

Jack launches himself into his arms. "I've had these strange feelings since we met, and I didn't know what they meant until now."

Tears fill Alex's eyes as he returns the embrace.

"Well, isn't that wonderful, Gladys!" Earl exclaims. "The pizza guy is my grandson's real father."

I start to laugh, and soon, everyone is laughing with me. Alex reaches for me and pulls me into his arms. This is the strangest day ever. I wipe a tear from my eye. "It's getting late. Why don't you take your son home? I'll meet you there when I'm done here."

"My first parental responsibility."

"I think you're up to the task." I lean in and kiss him. "Are you sure you're okay with all this information? Are you not freaked out at all?"

"Surprisingly, I'm not. Deep down, I knew it the whole time. I think that's why I sponsored all the sports in town."

"So, you'd have an excuse to come to watch him play." I fidget with the buttons on his shirt. "If you felt that way, why didn't you contact me?"

"You looked like you were happy and doing well. I didn't want to cause problems by hitting you with my crazy gut feeling."

"I suppose there's still lots to talk about."

"We'll figure it out. I don't expect we'll solve seventeen years of problems in one day."

I smile. "Why did you wait so long to come back to me."

"I didn't know you were waiting for me."

"See? Unfinished business," my mother adds as I roll her toward the elevator.

"Do you want us to walk you to your room, Earl?"

"No, thank you. I'm fine. I'm going to watch television before I go to sleep."

This time, the elevator stops on the fifth floor like it should. "You have a great night. I'll probably see you tomorrow." I roll the wheelchair into the hall.

"Goodbye, dear. Thank you for including me. It was quite an exciting day."

The elevator door closes, and my mom sighs. "I don't know what will happen to Earl when I die. I'm his only friend."

"Doesn't he have family? Besides Ryan?" I unlock the door and roll her into her apartment.

"He says sometimes he sees his son but no one else. Please, Maya, promise me you'll visit Earl after I go. I don't want him to be alone either."

"Okay, mom. I promise." I help her prepare for bed and glance at her bare finger as I pull her nightie over her head. "Did you ever find your wedding ring?"

224

Fear washes over her face.

"It's okay, Mom. If you misplaced it, I'm sure it will show up eventually. I was just wondering."

The last few days are the happiest I've seen her in a long while, but she struggles to get settled for bed. Every slight movement requires tremendous effort. I've been in denial about how quickly the disease is progressing. It's getting worse, much quicker than we expected. I try to be thankful that the medications seem to be doing their job and that she can have some quality of life without pain.

Within moments, she's asleep. I tidy a few things and gather up her laundry before I go.

While waiting for the elevator, I dispose of a trash bag in the waste room. It seems like forever for the elevator to arrive, and when the door opens, Ryan is in there, casually leaning against the back wall.

I'm surprised to see him. "Hi! You disappeared earlier."

"I work some unusual shifts, but I just wanted to come back and make sure he settled for the night."

"Your dad had a great time today. We played pool and fed him pizza. I hope he doesn't regret it now. We enjoyed his company."

"I'm glad. Most of his friends have passed, and until your mom moved in, he spent most of his time sitting in his room. He doesn't even know *I'm* here most of the time."

"Is his dementia getting worse? Is there nothing they can do to slow it down?"

"The specialists are doing everything they can. Some days, you wouldn't know he has it. Other days, he hallucinates and becomes very confused."

"I'm sorry."

"It is what it is. So, are you and the real estate guy going to give it another try?"

I find myself amused. "Why is everyone so concerned about Alex and me?"

"Because everybody should have someone. Love wouldn't be a great reward if there were no risks. There are no guarantees that love will last forever, Maya. But if you don't take a chance, it's guaranteed you won't know love at all."

"Very wise advice."

"I won't be around tomorrow," he says as he steps off the elevator in the lobby. "I've got some preparation to do for a special journey."

"You're going away?"

"I didn't think I'd be able to take this trip for a very long time. Plans have been in motion for some time now, but things are finally starting to line up and fall into place."

He's piqued my curiosity, but he stops at the front desk before I can ask more questions.

"I'd walk you to your car, but I need to talk to the manager about the sprinkler system on the third floor. I don't think it's working properly."

"Always on duty, huh?"

"Guilty."

"I'm surprised you haven't got the thing with the faulty fire alarm sorted out. The one in your dad's apartment goes off for no reason."

He gives me a mysterious grin. "Don't worry. That will sort itself out soon."

What a strange guy, I think to myself on the way home.

"Mom!" Jack screams, rushing to the door as soon as I open it.

"Whoa! What's going on?"

"I've got some great news!"

I put my keys on the hall table and follow him into the other room. Alex kisses me hello. "So, what's the great news?"

"I was talking to Jocelyn online a little while ago. She told me that some second cousin on her mom's side was tested a couple of days ago, and she's a match. She will get her procedure tomorrow, and there's a high probability of success."

"That is fantastic news. Does she know that you're not her brother?"

"Yeah, I broke that news to her. She was sad, but she said we can still be friends."

"I'm very proud of you, Jack. A lot of shit has gone down in the past few weeks, and you've handled it like a champ."

"I'm going to join an online game in my room. I was waiting to give you the news."

He runs up the stairs, leaving me hanging. "Thanks, Mom. I love you." I answer myself. Alex laughs.

"Well." I flop down on the couch. "It's the good news day that keeps on giving."

"It's not over yet."

"It's not?"

"Nope. I have something for you."

"You do? You brought me a present?"

"I did."

"Where is it?"

He reaches over the back of the couch, and I squint my eyes curiously. "What is that?" I ask as he lifts it. I reach out and take the unusually light roll out of his hand. "Is this bubble wrap?"

He breaks into a wide grin. "I'LL BEAT YOU UPSTAIRS!"

Chapter Twenty

The next day, I run errands, do chores around the house, and pick up groceries. It's no easy feat since Alex kept me awake all night, and I'm exhausted. By the time I arrive at Montgomery Gates, I can't find my mother. She's not in her room or the dining area. I panic as I approach the front desk and wait while they look through their records to see if they have taken her to any appointments. Suddenly, I hear the theme from *Mission: Impossible* coming up the hallway from the community activities room.

I breathe a sigh of relief as Jack wheels my mother around the corner into the lobby, using various descriptive sound effects. Earl is by their side.

He stops when he sees my look of disapproval. "I wish you had told me you were coming to visit," I scold. "I was having an anxiety attack wondering where everybody was." I shouldn't complain about him visiting. My mom looks twenty years younger today. "Did you at least stay out of trouble?"

"Gram's Amazon delivery came this morning, and she kicked my ass in a game of pool."

My eyes open wide in surprise. "Good for her."

Earl gives me a look of concern. "I think she might have overdone it."

"There's lots of time to rest when I'm dead," she says loudly.

All the residents within earshot nod their heads, making me laugh.

Jack taps me on the shoulder with the persistence of a toddler. "Mom, Mom! I know what I want to go to college for."

"You do?" I ask, surprised.

"Mr. MacDonald..." he begins.

"Who?"

"Earl."

"Oh, okay."

"Grandad." Earl corrects.

"Anyway," Jack continues, "He's been explaining how elevators work, and I think it's fascinating, so I looked it up online while we were playing pool. There's a course offered at the college in Oshawa. I wouldn't even have to live in residence."

"Slow down, chief. You're living in residence."

"Okay, we can negotiate that. But I was reading some articles on careers in Canada, and elevator inspector is one of the highest paying jobs," he says, vibrating with enthusiastic energy.

"Let's go eat, and you can tell me more about it."

"We already ate," my mom announces.

I feel the disappointment wash over me. "Oh."

"I'm going to hang around with Grams and..." he pauses and looks to me for help, but I shrug. "Grandad," he finishes reluctantly. "He's going to show me some tricks of the trade they don't teach you in school."

Earl stands proud. "We're kind of like kindred spirits."

"See? We're all good here, so you can leave," my mother says harshly.

I'm taken aback. "Excuse me?"

"You know...find something else to do?" Jack says with an exaggerated expression.

I stroll over to stand beside my son and lean in discretely. "What is going on?"

"Just go with it," he whispers.

"You should call Alex," Earl suggests.

"Yes," my mom agrees. "Go for a coffee or have dinner with someone your age. You're cramping our style. We're going to hang out with our peeps at Bingo."

"I hope they have better chocolate bars this time," Earl complains.

"Why look! It's Alex," Jack says, looking past me.

I turn to find him behind me, dressed in faded denim jeans and a casual plaid shirt. "What are you doing here?"

"Your mom left me a message saying she had questions about the house offer."

I turn and give her a curious glare.

"Oh, that," she says in an innocuous tone. She waves her hand in the air. "I already answered my question. Sorry about that, but since you're here, why don't you two go out and have a nice night?"

Alex narrows his eyes. "Why do I feel like this was a well-planned ambush?"

"No idea," Earl says innocently.

"Because it was," I confirm. "But I had no part in it."

He leans in to whisper in my ear. "Don't they know we're already a couple?"

I shrug. "I thought so, but now I'm confused."

"Wait. Why is Jack here? Shouldn't you be in school?"

"I'm taking a break to do some *grandsitting*. The opposite of *babysitting*."

Alex turns to me for clarification. "We have an agreement that he can have some flexibility in his school schedule to spend some time with his grandma if I get regular confirmation from his teachers that his work is done and at his usual level."

A grin forms on Alex's lips as he turns to me. "So, you're free tonight?"

"Apparently."

"Perfect, there's a new movie at the theatre I'd like to see."

I hold a finger in the air, pausing him. "Or, we can pick up some more bubble wrap and stay home."

Jack throws his hands over his ears. "Gah! Don't make it weird."

"Sorry," I laugh. "I'm not really sorry. You had it coming. You have been teasing me for weeks."

"Please," Jack begs. "Just go."

"That's our cue," Alex says, taking my hand.

A conversation at the front desk catches my attention.

"It's bizarre," one of the housekeeping girls says. "Every day for the past month, I've had to clean up ash and soot that mysteriously shows up in the stairwell, and we've had staff complain about their eyes burning and a strange campfire smell. Today, there's nothing."

"I know," one of the volunteers adds. "And suddenly, all the weirdness with the elevator has stopped."

A girl joining from the dining room jumps in. "And the fire alarms haven't gone off once all day."

I slow my pace so I can hear the conversation.

"I don't know why it's stopped, but I'm glad it has." The manager watches me as I pass, locking her eyes on mine and halting the conversation until I'm out of earshot.

"Did you hear that?" I ask Alex as he ushers me through the parking lot and into the car.

"I did."

"Don't you find it odd?"

"What I find odd is that those things were happening in the first place. Not that they've stopped."

Alex pulls out onto the road and then unexpectedly turns towards the lake. "Why are we stopping here?"

"I thought we could walk to our favourite spot."

"I haven't done that in..."

"More than seventeen years."

I smile. The setting sun sparkles on the water. "We had our first kiss here."

"This is where you stole my heart, Maya Dunn."

We sit on a bench and hold hands. It should have been a romantic moment, but I'm still fixated on the mystery.

"Yesterday, my mom made me promise that after she dies, we will continue to visit Earl."

"Really?"

I nod. "She says he has nobody, and she doesn't want him to be alone."

"That's sad. What did you say?"

"I told her I would, of course."

"Of course you did. I'd expect nothing else from you. You're a kind and unselfish person."

He stares at me with a look of adoration that makes me self-conscious. "What are you thinking?"

"How would you feel about changing the living arrangement?"

"How?"

"I was hoping you'd be open to us all living together under one roof. It doesn't matter if it's your place or mine. Or maybe we sell our current houses and buy something without history for either of us."

I'm suddenly reminded of something I overheard at Montgomery Gates about how the strange occurrences started happening shortly after Earl moved in. Is it just a coincidence?

"Hello? Earth to Maya."

"Sorry, what were you saying?"

"Where are you right now?"

"I'm here. With you."

"Are you sure? Because I'm trying to ask you something important here." He reaches into his pocket and pulls out a small blue box.

My heart starts to flutter. "What are you doing?"

He rakes his fingers through his hair and then exhales his nervousness in a single breath. "I've been holding on to this for seventeen years." He opens the box to expose the most beautiful ring I've ever seen. Its sparkle pales in comparison to his eyes right now.

"Everyone is right. We have unfinished business. I can't make up for all the time we lost, but I promise to do my best to make sure you're happy for the rest of our days." He takes the ring out of the box and reaches for my hand. It trembles slightly. "Will you marry me?"

"I don't know why the universe kept us apart and brought us back together at this particular time, but I know deep in my soul this is how it was always meant to be."

"So that's a yes, then?" he asks impatiently.

I can't stop smiling. "That's an absolute, yes."

He slides the ring on my finger, and my heart is so overfilled with joy that it could burst at any moment. I hold up my hand and watch the diamond sparkle. "I can't wait to tell Jack!"

"Oh. About that." He pulls his phone out of his pocket.

"Congratulations!" Jack screams through the phone.

I hear my mother in the background. "It's about time, Maya. I'm very happy for you, dear."

I narrow my eyes. "Have they been listening the whole time?"

Alex disconnects the call. "I'm sorry. I asked Jack for his blessing, and it was part of our agreement."

"Agreement?" I ask, shocked. "As in, you had to negotiate my hand in marriage with my son?"

Alex scratches his head. "Yeah."

"Wait. What did you mean by *part* of your agreement? He made you promise other things?"

"A few." He chuckles.

"Like what?" I demand.

"I'll tell you later. Let's not ruin this beautiful moment."

I look around us as the sun begins to set. There's suddenly an uptick in questionable activity in the area. "I think we should get out of here before it gets dark. Your beautiful moment is about to turn sketchy."

Alex smiles as we return to the car. "I agree. Things sure have changed around here." He opens the door and waits until I'm in. "Luckily, we have the house all to ourselves."

"So, we're not going to the movies?" I ask, disappointed. "I was looking forward to the popcorn."

"I'll make popcorn in the microwave afterwards."

"It's not the same as the movie popcorn." I pout. "I thought when you get older, sex isn't as important as doing things together and enjoying each other's company?"

He glances at me as he pulls into the driveway. "Until we're at that point, I want sex. If you're still thinking about popcorn after I'm done with you, then I haven't done my job right. I'm going to warn you now, I'm considering it a personal challenge tonight."

Chapter Twenty-One

Alex wraps his arms around me as I wash dishes at the sink. He buries his face in the crook of my neck and places gentle kisses there. "I have a showing this morning, but I'm free after that. Maybe we can talk about the housing situation?" His warm breath tickles my ear, and I pull away.

"What's wrong?"

"Would you be okay with a long engagement?"

"Why? Are you having second thoughts?"

"No. But don't you think we're moving too fast?"

"You think seventeen years is moving too fast?"

I frown. "I'm overthinking again."

"It's okay. Everything has been on fast-forward for the last few weeks. We can wait until you're ready." He grins as I turn to face him.

"What?" I ask suspiciously.

"You weren't thinking about popcorn when I got done with you last night, were you?"

"I was too exhausted to think about anything after you were done last night. Honestly, I don't know where you get your stamina."

"Years of conserving energy," he jokes.

"Good lord, is this what our sex life will amount to when we're married? "Bad jokes and sports innuendos?"

Alex grabs an apple from the counter. "Probably."

"I'll message you when I know what the plan is today. I want to check on my mom at some point."

"Send me a text."

He leans in for a kiss, and a group of muscles I'd forgotten I had until last night protests when I reach for him. I try to hide how sore I am, but a small groan escapes my lips.

Alex walks away with a victorious grin and runs into Jack on his way out. "Hey, bud. Are we on to conquer the final level of the new game tonight?"

"Absolutely."

"I'll catch up with you later."

Jack wanders into the kitchen, lured there by the smell of bacon.

"Thank you for keeping your grandma company last night. Alex and I needed the night off."

He reaches to steal food off the plate. "Now I know bacon is my reward, I'll offer to help more often."

"I can't believe you guys staged that whole thing yesterday."

"Grams and Earl were so excited about it. They practiced what they were going to say all morning."

"I had no clue what was going on. I thought you'd all lost your minds."

"Well, that is a true statement for some in attendance at the performance."

I smile. "You're a good kid. She looked so happy. I'll never talk her into coming to live with us now."

"I doubt it. She's making friends and having fun. Why would she want to live here?"

"Good point. Did you have fun after we left?"

"Grandma wasn't feeling well, so we took her to her room. I stayed with her until the nurse came to check her out. She said everything was normal, so she was probably just worn out from all the excitement."

"What did you do for the rest of the evening?"

"I hung out at my friend's house. I sent you a text message. Didn't you see it? The craziest thing happened when I got home. There were crows. Hundreds of crows just sitting in our front yard."

"That's creepy. My ringer must be turned off. As I reach for my phone, it vibrates in my hand. I look at the call number, and I'm immediately concerned that it's Montgomery Gates. "Good Lord, what kind of trouble did you three get into last night?"

Jack raises his shoulders, looking innocent. "If they're looking for us to pay damages, my name is Sven, and I don't speak English." Leaning against the counter, he steals another slice of bacon while he waits for me to take the call.

I laugh once as I answer. "Hello?" I listen and stand completely stunned in the middle of the kitchen with my phone pressed to my ear. I try to talk, but words get stuck in my throat. I disconnect the call and stare at my son with excruciating sorrow.

He stands erect. "Mom?" he says, concerned.

My heart beats like a drum in my chest. "She's gone."
I tuck my phone into my pocket, trying to maintain control.
"We have to go."

"I'll call Alex," Jack says as I walk in a daze down the
hall and pick up my keys.

"Mom? Are you okay to drive?"

"I'm fine," I assure him.

There's a strange quiet in the lobby of Montgomery
Gates as I watch the coroner roll his gurney out of the
elevator and outside to the waiting hearse. I hold Jack tightly
as he weeps. Residents offer us their condolences as they
come and go from the dining room. Every staff member and
volunteer offers a sympathetic smile.

I move toward the elevator, and Jack pauses. "I'll wait
down here for Alex."

I nod, knowing that he needs to see him right now.

The door to her room is still propped open. Residents
peek out from their doorways as I stand there frozen. I finally
find the strength to step in.

Feeling lost, I tidy the room and mentally note the
personal items I'll need to pack up. Her spirit has barely left
this world, but I don't know what else to do with myself right
now. Suddenly, emotion hits me hard, and I plop myself down
on the side of the bed. The air around me becomes heavy,
making it hard for me to breathe. The mattress beside me
dips like someone has just sat beside me on the bed. I feel a

240

chilling sensation on my cheek, and I know I've just received a frosty kiss. I bury my face in my cold, shaking hands as I break into a hard sob, and I'm magically surrounded by an energy that I can't explain.

I hear Alex whisper as he crosses the room. "Maya."

I take a stuttered breath as he sits beside me, and his weight sinks the mattress further, causing me to slide toward him. He surrounds me with his arms and anchors me against his chest. "I came as soon as I got Jack's message."

I look around the room. "Where is he?"

"He's downstairs having a hot chocolate. He'll come up when he's ready." He rests his forehead against mine in silent support before pressing his lips to the top of my head. "I'm so sorry."

"She's in a better place," I try to convince myself.

He holds me safely in the crook of his neck. "She is."

A strange feeling that someone is watching me prompts me to look up. Ryan stands eerily silent in the doorway. His figure is dark, intense...haunting. A ghost of a smile forms on his lips, and he gives me a slight nod in acknowledgement.

Alex strokes my hair, drawing away my attention. "Is there anything we need to do?"

When I look again...Ryan is gone. "They're taking her to the funeral home. I need to take the bag with her clothes there."

"Okay, where's the bag?"

"I shoved it under the bed out of the way."

"I'll get it," Jack says as he joins us.

I get to my feet and begin opening drawers and moving stuff around, desperately seeking the lost jewelry.

"What are you looking for?" Jack asks. "I can help you look."

"I was looking for her wedding ring. I noticed she wasn't wearing it after telling me Jennifer had visited. I asked her if she gave it to her, but she couldn't remember what she did with it."

"If Grandma left it to you in her will, won't she have to return it?"

"If she took it, I guarantee she's sold it by now."

I give up and push the final drawer closed. "I don't know how long we have to move her stuff out."

Alex rubs my shoulder. "Thirty days. I asked before I came up."

"So, I don't need to worry about that right now."

"No. You have plenty of time to plan the funeral and mourn her loss before we have to start boxing up anything."

I look at him, panicked, and he knows what I'm thinking.

"Don't worry, sweetheart. She signed everything, so the sale is legal, and the money will be sent to her estate through her lawyer on the closing date."

I close my eyes and take a breath. "Then there's nothing else to do today but drop this bag off and start making calls."

"I'm here to help you with anything you need."

Jack paces anxiously around the small space. "Before we go, Mom, can we see Mr. MacDonald? I think I should be the one to tell him."

"Of course."

Alex grabs the key from the peg beside the door. "You're going to need this." He locks the door behind us while Jack presses the elevator button.

"What's taking so long?" Alex asks when he joins us.

"It looks like the elevator is stuck on the sixth floor."

"I'm done waiting," Jack says impatiently. "I'm taking the stairs."

"It's only one flight up," Alex reasons. "Are you up to it?"

"I'll manage."

Jack waits for us at the top of the stairwell. The door to Earl's room is ajar, so Jack knocks once and then sticks his head in. "Mr. MacDonald?"

He looks up and smiles. "Do I know you?"

Jack glances over at me, confused. "He doesn't recognize me?"

I frown. "His son told me his dementia was getting worse, and the medication was doing little to help." From his distant look and confusion, it's clear that today is not a good day.

Jack nods his understanding. "Yes. We're friends."

He nods as his brow furrows. "I remember. We played pool." He turns to me with a stoic expression. "Your mother is gone now."

I nod. "Yes, she passed away this morning."

"The elevator is stuck on this floor again."

"Yes, Alex called the front desk to let them know."

The smoke alarm lets out an eerie noise and then stops. We exchange an uneasy look.

"No one will figure out what's wrong with that elevator. It's possessed." Earl lowers his eyes.

I walk toward him and notice a family picture hanging on the wall. He was much younger then, but the resemblance between the father and son is uncanny. He watches me curiously.

"Did you know my son, Ryan?"

"I did. We've had many chats. I want to let him know about my mom and say goodbye."

Confusion washes over him, and he becomes agitated. "You're a few months late for the funeral."

I raise a brow and look over my shoulder at Jack. "Funeral?"

"He was a hero," Earl says proudly. "The whole town came out to the cemetery to say goodbye."

"I think you're confused. I had lunch with you and Ryan two days ago," I remind him.

His blank stare begins to heighten my emotions. "Earl? I saw Ryan downstairs a few minutes ago. Did he come to see you today?"

His eyes well up with tears.

"Mom," Jack interrupts. I look at him, and he directs my attention to a framed newspaper on the other side of the room. I walk toward it and read the five-month-old headline.

Beneath it is a picture of Ryan in his firefighter uniform and the funeral details. My heart begins to pound heavily, and I forget to breathe momentarily. Alex places his hand on my shoulder and gives it a gentle squeeze. "How is this possible?" I whisper as I tilt my head and brush my cheek against his knuckles.

"Some things can't be explained."

I glance at the elderly gentleman and remember one of the last things Ryan said to me and my promise to my mom. "Maybe not, but I think I understand. There were higher powers at work here." I cross the room and reach down to touch Earl's hand. "Have you had lunch yet today?"

He raises his eyes to mine. "No, I haven't had much of an appetite today."

"Well, I'm starving. Would you go down and have lunch with us?" A glimmer in his eye washes away the empty feeling I've had deep inside since I got the call.

"If it's not too much trouble."

"Not at all," Alex adds, extending his hand to help him to his feet. "Let's hope they have that elevator fixed."

"No such luck," Jack says, opening the door. We'll have to take the service elevator down. We take a long, slow walk at Earl's pace down the hall. I pull my sweater around me, trying to keep warm. "This place is always so drafty and cold."

As we round the corner, a tall man walking with an elderly woman comes into view. Lights flicker as they pass beneath them, and I feel uneasy and anxious. I know them. Earl shuffles his feet as quickly as he can, but they are way ahead of us, and my eyes can't focus on the distance in the dim light. As they reach the elevator, my body tenses.

"Maya? Are you okay?" Alex asks, concerned.

"Yeah, you and Jack keep walking with him. I'll hold the elevator." I take quick steps toward them. The closer I get, the more certain I am that I'm not seeing things. I'm only a few feet away when the elevator door opens, and they step in. "Wait!" I rush the last few steps and put my hand on the door to stop it from closing. My obstruction causes the door to reopen, and shock makes me gasp as I stand face-to-face with Ryan and my mother. I can't find my voice. I can't even comprehend what I'm seeing. A sweet, gentle smile forms on my mother's lips, and I can tell she's no longer in pain and finally at peace. "Ryan is taking me to see your father," she says in a loving, maternal tone. "We're not needed here anymore."

"Mom," I whisper.

"You'll be just fine. Nobody is alone anymore."

I begin to tremble and drop my hand to my side. The elevator button lights up, and the door starts to close.

"Wait," I beg, trying to delay their departure as the others approach.

"Sorry," Ryan says as the door begins to close. "We're going *up*."

Alex and Jack are stunned as they get a glimpse inside the elevator before the door closes and the green arrow points upward. Jack pushes the button several times, trying to force it to open.

"Aren't we on the top floor?" Alex asks, confused.

I purse my lips and hold back the tears. Tears of joy; tears of sorrow.

"I don't think they're taking the elevator to where they're going," Earl adds.

I give him a knowing smile. "I believe you're right. Something tells me he'll come back for you one day. When it's time."

Earl nods, and his expression lightens.

When the door opens a few moments later, it's empty. There's a faint scent of smoke and roses. I inhale deeply, trying to commit the smell to memory so I'll never forget. "I guess Ryan's unfinished business was to make sure his father won't be alone."

Jack smiles. "Grandma's unfinished business was to make sure Alex came back into our lives."

Alex wraps his arms around me as we make the journey to the main floor. "So, I just witnessed that?"

"That depends on what you think you saw," I jest.

He holds the door so it won't close as Jack helps Earl exit and guides him toward the dining room.

"We're all he has left in this world," I say as I pass. Alex stops me and gives me a chivalrous smile. "We'll make sure he won't spend the rest of his days alone."

Tears well up in my eyes. "Thank you for standing beside me through all this craziness."

Alex leans down and brushes a tender kiss on my lips. "I'm not going to lie. For a while, I thought the stress was getting to you. Nobody else saw Ryan but you."

"Until today," Jack adds. "I wonder why I never saw him?"

"I guess he only wanted to be seen by me."

The girl at the front desk calls out when she sees me. "Miss Dunn!"

"Yes?"

"Someone left an envelope for you."

"You go sit and save me a seat. I'll be right there." I walk toward her. "Who?"

"Nobody knows. It was just sitting here on the desk this morning."

She picks up a bulgy envelope stained with a dark smudge. "It had to be one of the residents or the night staff. It wasn't here when I locked the front doors last night."

"I don't recognize the writing." I take it out of her hand, and a distinct scent hits me. I lift it to my nose as I join the boys in the dining room. "Smell this." I pass it to Alex as I sit down.

"It smells like smoke." He passes it to Jack. "Does this smudge look like soot to you?"

"It does."

I take it out of his hand. "Let's see what's inside." I tear the top off the soiled envelope and dump the contents into my hand. Everyone watches curiously as ash and rose petals pour into my palm, forming a pile. As the envelope empties, something heavy drops, forcing ash and dust upwards into the air.

Jack squints his eyes. "What is it?"

I smile and pull a sparkling band from beneath a petal. "It's my mother's wedding ring."

A mysterious breeze in the middle of the indoor dining room causes the ash and dust to swirl upward from my hand and disappear into thin air. No one speaks. We don't have to. My mother told stories of how the magic of Ireland lives in us. Not one of us can deny it now.

Epilogue

Rose bushes flourish and bloom around the fence line of our new home. Determined to look forward, we chose a home that is perfect for us.

Today, the trellis in the back garden is decorated for the occasion, and the rose bushes we transplanted from my parent's original garden are finally thriving, as if the magic has returned.

A small gathering is what we planned. Only a few of our most treasured and trusted friends will join us; my siblings didn't make the list.

I decided it was fitting, and funny as hell, to wear the dress from the awards dinner on our wedding day. I'm determined to get my money's worth out of this damn dress. I spend all morning getting ready, and it's finally time.

Chairs in the yard are organized into small rows with a path to the trellis down the centre. At the front, two chairs are marked reserved on both sides of the aisle.

All our guests are seated, and before we begin, Earl and I have something to do. "Are you ready?" I ask, reaching out my hand.

"I am."

Earl and I walk through the yard and stop in front of two reserved chairs. Earl places Ryan's Ontario Medal of

Firefighter Bravery on one chair, and I place my mother's wedding ring, tied to a long-stem rose, on the other.

"Do you think they're here?" Earl asks in an emotional tone.

I squeeze his arm. "I'm positive they are," I assure him.

"Well, what are you waiting for? Get married!"

A large black crow lands on the fence. I give it a menacing look, but it ignores me and ruins the peaceful afternoon with its cawing. "Hold that thought," I say to Earl as I pick up the shovel Jack left in the garden and walk toward the fence.

"Mom!" Jack yells.

Startled, I stop in my tracks.

Jack reaches my side and discreetly removes the shovel from my hand. "Were you really going to hit it with the shovel in front of all these people?"

I look around the yard. "Bad idea?"

"Yes, bad idea. Although, I have this strong feeling that Grams is laughing right now."

"Probably because she told me to do it. Is Alex ready?"

"He's been ready for seventeen years."

I straighten his tie. "You look so handsome. Let's do this."

I sneak around the back of the chairs and stand out of sight while Alex and Earl walk down the aisle toward the officiant. Earl shakes Alex's hand and sits in one reserved spot.

When the music starts, Jack takes my arm and escorts me down the aisle. Stopping in front of the trellis, he hugs me and then shakes Alex's hand before sitting beside Earl.

Alex faces me and holds my hands. His expression mirrors the adoration I'm feeling. "I didn't think you could look more beautiful than the first time I saw you in that dress, but you're absolutely glowing."

The officiant says a few words about love and relationships. I'm so fixated on the sparkle in Alex's eyes that I couldn't repeat a single word from the service. The entire world ceases to exist until I hear the words. "You may kiss the bride."

A warm wind picks up and swirls around the yard, causing movement throughout the garden. In a hushed tone, I hear somebody say they smell smoke as Alex brings his lips to mine in a romantic display of our love and devotion.

Like the symbolic entwined branches of the ancient Celtic tree of life, our souls become irrevocably interconnected and dependent on each other for survival.

An ethereal voice whispers the Irish word for *soft breeze* in my ear, and suddenly, rose petals from around the garden are gently carried upward in a stream of air around us. They move freely in all directions, falling from the sky and floating to the ground.

Alex laughs at the strange phenomenon as he holds out his hand, trying to catch some of the fragile petals. As the warm air surrounding us becomes infused with the distinct apple fragrance of the fairy rose, I feel overjoyed.

When I glance at Jack, there are tears in his eyes. He nods his acknowledgement. It's not just those of us with *a gift* who knows our loved ones are with us today.

About the Series

There is no place more beautiful to me than the home I've made with the love of my life. We're surrounded by rushing waters, rugged landscapes, rolling hills and magnificent views. Where people are real, and life doesn't have to be perfect to be wonderful. It's the most magnificent inspiration for love. Inspired by the communities that form the Headwaters, the 'Love in the Hills of the Headwaters Series' will bring you stories you can relate to; people you can connect with; and love you can believe in. It's the perfect place for city glam to meet country charm. Come Join us in the Hills of the Headwaters and find a place to explore, unplug and fall in love.

About the Author

Tricia Daniels was born and raised in the suburbs of Toronto, Ontario. 30 years ago, she moved to a small town in Dufferin County where she raised three sons as a single mother. The happily-ever-after she thought she would never have took her by surprise when she met her one great love, later in life. Love changes everything and Tricia Daniels strives to bring you love stories you can relate to.